BULL

THE BUCK BOYS HEROES SERIES

DEBORAH BLADON

FIRST ORIGINAL EDITION, 2021

Copyright © 2021 by Deborah Bladon

All rights reserved. No parts of this book may be reproduced in any form or by any means without written consent from the author.

This is a work of fiction. Names, characters, places and incidents either are the product of the author's imagination or are used fictitiously. Any resemblance to actual person's, living or dead, events, or locales are entirely coincidental.

eBook ISBN: 9781926440675
ISBN: 9798770435115

Book & cover design by Wolf & Eagle Media

deborahbladon.com

CHAPTER ONE

Trina

"WE'VE MET, HAVEN'T WE?"

I turn at the sound of the unfamiliar voice to my left. It's a dark-haired woman, at least twice my age, with frown lines near the corners of her mouth and a sparkle in her green eyes.

I shake my head. "I don't think so."

"Are you sure?" She leans closer. The smell of peppermint mixed with a citrus-scented perfume emanates from her. "I swear that I know you."

Her gaze slides over me from head to toe, taking in the white blouse and black skirt I'm wearing.

"I have one of those faces." I smile.

It's the same line I always use when a stranger approaches me to ask if we know each other. I've been mistaken countless times for a salesperson at Macy's or a first-grade elementary teacher. Once, a man was convinced that I was his server at a diner in the Theater District.

"You work at the library, don't you?" She tilts her head.

"The main branch. I was in there last week. You were behind the counter."

A blonde with blue eyes and hair styled in a tight bun might have been, but I haven't been to the New York Public Library in years. The last time was with my mom when I was ten or eleven years old.

My guess is that she's been to my family's bakery in Brooklyn. The walls are covered with framed photographs of my twelve siblings and me.

A man sprinting to catch the light to cross the street knocks my elbow in his rush to get past me. I stumble forward on the sidewalk, but I manage to stay upright with quick work of my feet.

"Watch it, asshole!" The woman I've been talking to yells after him. "It's illegal to hurt a librarian."

It's wrong to run into anyone and not apologize.

I don't have time to debate that. I need to get to work before my boss does, and since I've only made it a block from my apartment, I have to sprint to the subway so I won't be late.

I turn to the woman who defends librarians. "I should go."

"I'll be at the library again soon." She glances at her watch. "I'll be sure to stop by and say hello."

I'll be behind my desk in an office far from there.

Correcting this woman would be the right thing to do, but I don't want to embarrass her, and I don't have an extra minute to spare.

"I'm Beth, by the way." She offers her hand.

I take it in mine. "My name is Trina."

That sets her back a step. "Trina. That suits you."

I like that she thinks so, so I smile. "Thank you."

Beth glances over my shoulder. "There's the friend I'm meeting. I'll see you again, Trina."

I watch as she subtly slips the gold band from the ring finger on her left hand before she deposits it in the pocket of her jacket. Her smile widens as she lifts her now bare hand to wave at the man approaching us.

I doubt I'll ever see Beth again, but I have to wonder if the man who put that ring on her finger knows what she's doing this Tuesday morning. It's just one of the many secrets the millions of people in New York City hold close.

My thoughts are interrupted when my phone starts ringing. I hunt through my purse before I pull it out.

Cringing, I see my boss's name flash across the screen.

I answer immediately. "Good morning, Mr. Locke. How are you today, sir?"

"Busy," he says brusquely in that toe-curling deep voice of his. "I'm stopping by the office to pick up my notes for my meeting with Mr. Tillery this morning. I expect those to be on my desk when I arrive in thirty minutes, Miss Shaw."

Well, shit.

Hurrying to the corner, I wave my hand in the air, frantically searching for an available taxi.

"I'll have that ready for you," I say, hoping that I'm predicting the future.

"Fine." He ends the call just like that because that's how Graham Locke rolls. He's all business, no politeness.

I silently fist pump the air when a taxi slows. I'll beat Mr. Locke to the office with time to spare.

Opening the back passenger door of the taxi, I catch one last glimpse of Beth in the arms of the man she's hiding her wedding ring from. I glance at my left hand. It's void of any jewelry. One day I hope a man will slide a ring on my finger, and if our love is true and strong, it will stay there until I take my very last breath on this earth.

———

"WHAT IS THIS?"

Those three little words hold so much punch in my world.

Mr. Locke likes to fire them at me whenever I do something that isn't up to his standards.

Case in point:

I ordered lunch for him one day last week. The mustard on the rye bread was of the regular yellow variety because the restaurant ran out of the gourmet whole grain type. Most people would be fine with that, but not my boss. Mr. Locke took one bite of the stacked ham and cheese overpriced monstrosity and spat it out into a napkin.

"What is this?" he barked at me.

I didn't bother to reply because it was a sandwich with the wrong mustard, not the end of civilization as we know it.

Today, the question is coming at me while he's holding the typed minutes of yesterday's staff meeting in his hands.

I look up at where he's standing in front of my desk.

Good looking is a subjective term except when it comes to Graham Locke. Everyone thinks he's firecracker hot. He's handsome in that *I-didn't-bother-trying* way some men are. Maybe it's his blue eyes and dark brown hair. I have no idea if his custom-tailored suits add to the allure, but I do know that if I didn't know him, I'd rate him a twelve out of ten.

When he opens his mouth, and his rudeness shines through, he drops a couple of notches on my attraction meter.

I clear my throat and speak the truth, "Those are the minutes from yesterday's meeting, sir."

Wrong answer.

I see that immediately in the way he tosses his '*what the fuck?*' look in my direction. It's a combination of a scowl and a shake of his head.

"I don't need to reread the mundane details of what everyone did last weekend." He throws the papers on my desk with a flick of his wrist. "I heard it once and didn't care enough to remember any of it, including your date on Friday night."

Well boo.

I paste a sweet smile on my face and look up at him. "All of that was part of the meeting."

"All of that is frivolous and unnecessary," he counters. "Rewrite the minutes without any of that included."

I thought the details of my date were compelling. My co-workers seemed to think so too. It was a second date, so they're invested in what's happening between Kyle, my kind of almost-boyfriend, and me.

"I'll work on that now," I say, going for another overly forced smile.

"Complete it within the hour."

I'm up for the challenge, so I put the pedal to the metal, or in my case, my fingers to the keyboard, and get to work cutting out the best parts of yesterday's meeting so that I can hand the boring document over to the worst boss in New York City.

CHAPTER TWO

Trina

THREE WEEKS Later

"ARE you saying I'll never get to meet Kyle?" My neighbor, Aurora Salik, shakes her head. "I was looking forward to checking out his ass."

I bark out a laugh. "His ass? Why?"

"Did you not say that he had an ass that was so tight you could bounce quarters off of it?"

Still chuckling, I take a seat next to her small dining room table. "Kyle's ass wasn't worth talking about."

"Oh," she draws the word out slowly. "I bet you were talking about your boss's ass when you said that."

It's likely, but I won't admit it.

"Back to my breakup with Kyle," I say to shift the subject away from Mr. Locke's spectacular ass. "He wasn't impressed that I didn't know how to play chess."

"Wow. You lost a keeper, didn't you?"

I smile.

This feels good.

I've known Aurora for a little more than a year. She was already living in this apartment with her boyfriend, Eldon, when I moved in down the hall.

They both welcomed me with open arms.

Since then, we've become friends.

"I'm not crying over it," I confess.

When Kyle told me last week that he wanted to date someone with the same interests as him, I hightailed it out of the restaurant before the server brought the check. I figured that Kyle owed me one last dinner and a drink since I sat through his retelling of every aspect of the history lesson he taught his class of eighth-graders that day.

I'm all for diving into the past, but not on a fifth date.

If Kyle hadn't pulled the plug on our blossoming relationship that night, I would have done it myself.

"Good." Aurora pats my hand before she takes a long drink from the mug in front of her.

She works at a café, so her coffee-making skills are next level. When she texted me fifteen minutes ago to say that she made me a cup, I knocked on her apartment door seconds later.

My gaze wanders to a framed picture on the wall behind her. It's a shot that was taken on a beach in Maryland last year on Aurora's twenty-first birthday. Her brown hair is blowing in the breeze. One of her hands is trying to control it while the other is on her boyfriend's shoulder as he gazes into her eyes.

"How's Eldon?"

"Handsome as ever." She beams. "What is it about a man in a uniform?"

I've seen Eldon Breckton in his NYPD uniform more than once. It's a good look for him.

"Eldon can set you up with someone from work," she offers with a glint in her eye. "Maybe a double date?"

I know better than to agree to go on a blind date. I've tried that in the past, and it's never worked out for me. I'd love to find the man I'm destined to spend my life with, but I'm only twenty-four, so I can pace myself.

Besides, if the blind date ends badly, that's a mark on my friendship with Aurora and Eldon that I don't want.

"Thanks, but I'm taking a break from dating."

The mug in her hand stops mid-air. "Because?"

"No reason in particular." I grin. "More me time, less he time."

"By '*he*' you mean every available man in Manhattan?"

"Exactly." I punctuate the word with a nod.

"I said that the day before I met Eldon." She takes a sip from her mug. "Look how that turned out for me."

"WHAT DO YOU THINK, TRINA?"

I look up from my desk to see Kay, one of our designers, with a massive man's silver watch on her wrist.

She's clinging to the band tightly while she admires her workmanship.

"I think Abdons has a new bestseller on their hands." I pause for effect. "Or should I say their wrists?"

She laughs the same way she always does when I crack that joke.

Kay has been working at Abdons for decades. She was one of the first employees when Lloyd Abdon launched his designer watch brand in a small shop on the Lower East Side.

The company has grown into a multi-million-dollar business since that day. Mr. Abdon still pops into the office whenever the urge strikes, but he handed over the day-to-day reins to Mr. Locke last year.

"Is he around?" Kay's gaze darts to Mr. Locke's closed office door.

He is, but he's in a grumpy mood.

I found that out when I chirped *"good morning"* to my boss, and his response was a shoot of death rays from his eyes in my direction.

That's a slight exaggeration, but it was apparent something or someone turned what could have been a good morning for him into an *angry a.m.*, as I call it. That's not to be confused with the *pissy p.m.* he has at least a few times a week.

"Mr. Locke is busy," I lie to save Kay from his wrath. "Why don't I check with him later to see when he's available?"

That's my polite way of saying that I'll wait until that ten-minute window each day when he's not about to cut someone's head off with his words.

"Works for me," she says in a tone edged with glee. "I think he's going to love my new design."

I think he'll say it's "fine" before instructing one of the new designers he hired to come up with something cutting edge with a host of bells and whistles.

Kay is still designing watches for people who only use their timepiece to *well*…tell time. Mr. Locke is trying to corner the market for those who want to call their business partners, book a lunch reservation, and plan their Aruba vacation from the comfort of their wrists.

"Back to the design lab for me." She turns abruptly and stomps off.

I watch her leave, wishing I could go with her because I know my boss, and twenty-five minutes from now, he'll swing open his office door and order me to get him a sandwich that will in no way satisfy him.

I glance at the vintage silver Abdons watch on my wrist.

Twenty-four minutes and fifty-seven seconds from now, the mid-day fun begins.

CHAPTER THREE

TRINA

I STEPPED out to get Mr. Locke his lunch, and he split.

He took off like a bat under the cover of darkness.

No one noticed him leave, not even Cecil at the reception desk, and he spots everything.

I look at the white paper bag in my hand.

Today's lunch order consisted of turkey, avocado, and arugula on whole grain bread with a zesty sauce and a sprinkle of pepper.

It smells delicious, and although I was tempted to order myself one, I pushed that notion aside because there's a bowl of macaroni salad in the fridge in the break room with my name on it.

Literally.

I wrote my name on the lid because Cecil is under the impression that the fridge is a buffet just for him. He picks and chooses his appetizer, entrée, and dessert from there almost every day.

I drop the bag on my desk and turn in a circle, looking for some inspiration.

Do I eat the sandwich or wait to hear from Locke?

The hunger gods must hear me because my phone chimes in my purse.

I dig it out.

My gaze drops to the screen to find a text message from the man himself.

> ***Mr. Locke:*** **I'll be out of the office for the remainder of the day. Reschedule my meetings.**

MY STOMACH GROWLS a response before I do.

> ***Trina:*** **Very well, sir.**

NOT ONLY WILL I be dining on a fourteen-dollar sandwich for lunch, but I'll make it home before dinnertime tonight.

I don't have plans. Well, unless you count organizing my utensil drawer as plans.

I take a seat behind my desk and grab a paper napkin from the stack I keep hidden in my bottom drawer.

That lands on my lap because I happen to like the skirt I'm wearing, and I don't want a splotch of zesty sauce to send it to the dry cleaners prematurely.

I carefully unwrap the sandwich like the gift that it is.

Just as I pick it up, my phone chimes again.

I close my eyes and make a wish that it's a text message from one of my twelve siblings because, on any given day, most of them reach out at least once.

My parents still insist on calling me from their landline.

Against my better judgment, I glance at my phone.

I read the text message on my screen. "What the fuck?"

That's followed by uncontrollable laughter because this has to be a joke.

Graham Locke is pranking me.

He must be because there is no way in hell that the words on my screen are real.

I read his text message again.

Mr. Locke: **Meet me at the City Clerk's office at 3 PM today for my wedding.**

"WHO WOULD MARRY YOU?" I blurt out.

My boss keeps his private life under wraps, but I can't imagine any woman wanting to marry him unless hot grump with good hair is a type.

I need clarification more than I need a bite of the sandwich, so I pick up my phone.

Trina: **You're getting married today?**

I FIRE that off without another thought.

Why do I care if he gets married today or any other day?

Feeling like I've suddenly lost my appetite, I wrap the sandwich back up and write my name across the bag in big, bold letters because I don't want Cecil to touch it.

I move to stand to head to the break room just as my phone chimes again.

I drop my gaze to the screen.

Mr. Locke: 3 PM at the City Clerk's office, Miss Shaw. DON'T BE LATE.

LOOKING at the watch on my wrist, I fall back on my chair.

Two hours and twenty-one minutes from now, I'll witness my boss marry a woman who has to be a saint.

Whoever the future Mrs. Locke is, I wish her luck. She may be marrying someone tagged one of *"The Most Gorgeous Men in Manhattan"* on an Instagram account I follow, but her soon-to-be husband is a jerk for the ages.

I hope she knows what she's getting into.

"THAT'S out of your price league," my brother says as he jerks his thumb to the left. "If you need bubbly, Trina, the discount bin is over there."

"Thanks, George." I flash him a grin. "This is a gift, so I'm going all out."

I'll say I am. This bottle of champagne I picked out as a

wedding gift for my boss and his wife is just shy of two hundred dollars.

I don't know the proper etiquette about showing up to a wedding without a gift in hand, but I think it's just plain rude.

Besides, Mrs. Locke is probably going to need a drink within a few hours after the ceremony.

My brother rings the purchase up in the cash register. "I'll toss in a gift bag at no charge."

"Gee, thanks." I smile.

George's store is my go-to place for anything alcoholic.

He doesn't give discounts to anyone, but he will toss in a free gift of some sort if he can.

I reach over to pluck a shiny silver bag from the bin next to the counter.

"Who is this for?" he asks warily. "Someone must be celebrating something important for you to invest this much in their gift."

George is the most protective of my siblings.

If I tell him that I'm buying this for my boss, he'll lecture me on how Graham's not worth it.

George has heard me moan enough times about Mr. Locke to know that he'll never win any Boss of the Year awards.

I hand him my credit card. "A wedding deserves a gift to remember."

"Someone's getting married?" He runs my card through the register. "Good for them. Marriage is the best decision I ever made."

"You're one of the lucky ones," I say to steer him toward talking about his wife.

He takes the bait.

As I tuck my credit card back into my purse, I listen to the story about his wedding day and how it was everything he always wanted it to be.

I only hope that when I get married, it's as perfect as his special day was.

CHAPTER FOUR

Trina

I RACE up the sidewalk toward the building that houses the City Clerk's office. I slow my pace when I spot Mr. Locke standing on the sidewalk a few feet in front of me.

Wowza.

The suit he's wearing is a three-piece dark blue number. He's got a light blue tie on that is knotted to perfection.

The future Mrs. Locke did luck out when it comes to having a photogenic husband. He'll look killer in every shot they take today, especially if he smiles.

I've witnessed that a few times.

It's always when a new location of Abdons opens. On those days, money signs must be dancing behind his eyes because he's borderline cheerful, or at the very least cordial.

Right now, he looks less than pleased.

Maybe I should have changed into something more suitable to witness his wedding. I have no clue what that would be.

I think the red blouse and black pencil skirt that I wore to work today will do the job just fine.

"Congratulations, sir!" I hold the gift bag in the air. My fingers are wrapped tightly around the twine handles because this is precious cargo.

"Right."

Huh?

It's his wedding day. The least he can do is crack open the smile vault and let one fly.

Someone needs to tell him that smiles don't cost a penny.

I look around. "Where's the bride? What's her name?"

He drags a hand through his perfectly styled hair.

Uh oh.

That move only happens when the world, as he knows it, is about to collapse. It happened that time he tasted regular mustard and the day I spilled coffee in his lap.

The heel on my shoe broke. I lunged forward. Lukewarm coffee landed on his thousand dollar pants. It was a whole thing.

His gaze darts to the left and then the right, but it doesn't seem as though he's looking for someone.

If he got stood up, I'm taking this champagne back to my brother's store for a refund.

Mr. Locke drops his hand and looks me in the eye. "You're her."

"Urher?" I repeat, not wanting to butcher his fiancée's name. "Am I pronouncing that right? Or is it with an accented e, like Urhér?"

He looks at me like my head is about to fall off.

I continue rambling because I'm on a roll, "It's a unique name. She must be lovely."

"You. Are. Her," he states each word slowly and with purpose. "You are marrying me."

"What?" I blurt out through a stuttered laugh. "What did you just say?"

His expression shifts, and a slight smile ghosts his lips. "I need you to marry me, Miss Shaw."

I feel my mouth fall open, but I do nothing to change that.

"I've called in a favor with a judge, so we're skipping the mandatory twenty-four-hour waiting period after we get the license." He glances down at the Abdons watch on his wrist. "The ceremony will happen as soon as we have the license in hand."

"Marriage license? Ceremony? A judge?" I toss out random words that have no right to be in my vocabulary at this moment in time.

"I need us to be married by tomorrow afternoon." He tilts his head. "There isn't an opening in my schedule tomorrow morning, so we have to move it if we're going to get this done before the City Clerk's office closes for the day."

I take a step back. "No."

"No?" he repeats it like it's a curse word.

"I'm not marrying you." My voice is edged with a chuckle because this is as preposterous as it gets.

Did he fall and hit his head in his rush to get out of the office earlier?

"We need to get married," he insists with another shove of his hand through his hair.

"We're not getting married," I argue. "Are you all right, sir? Are you feeling okay?"

"I'm frustrated," he admits as if it's not obvious.

A vein in his neck is pulsing. I catch sight of it every time I glance at his Adam's apple.

"Let's get you back to the office," I say in as calm a tone as I can muster. "Is there someone I can call for you?"

"Miss Shaw," he hisses my name out. "I need you to

marry me now. That is non-negotiable so tell me what I need to do to make it happen in the next…" He drops his gaze to his watch. "Thirty-eight minutes."

Steadying my feet on the pavement, I look him in the eye. "I'm not marrying you, sir."

"Because of Kyle?"

I don't know if I'm more stunned that Mr. Locke knows the name of the guy I briefly dated or that he thinks that would be the only reason barring me from marrying him.

"No. We broke up."

He rubs his jaw. "What's the issue then?"

Is that a trick question? I could list a million reasons why I won't dive into the marriage pool with him.

"Give me one good reason why you won't marry me," he begins as he glances at his watch again. "And make it quick."

"I don't like you."

No, no, no. I didn't let that slip out, did I?

"I'm not asking you to like me," he spits the last two words out with a smirk. "I'm asking you to marry me."

"I can't do that."

He grabs hold of my forearm to shuffle me out of the way of an approaching group of people.

My gaze searches his face. "Why do you want to marry me?"

He lets out a heavy exhale. "Mr. Abdon is coming to New York tomorrow. He's under the impression we're married."

I take in every word he just said. "Why would he be under that impression?"

His answer is quick and to the point. "I told him we got married."

My gaze follows his hand as he reaches into the front pocket of his pants. He pulls out a small white box.

When he pops it open, my breath catches because, *holy mother of all things sparkly*, that diamond is huge.

"If we hurry, we can have this done by the end of the day," he says as he shoves the box into my palm.

That's not going to win any awards for the most romantic proposal of the year.

I push the box back at him. "This is not happening. You need to tell Mr. Abdon the truth."

He lowers his voice. "I need you to tell me what it's going to take to get you to marry me, Miss Shaw. This is temporary and in name only. What do you want? One hundred thousand? A quarter of a million?"

"Dollars?" I screech. "Sir!"

"Five hundred thousand," he says in a rush. "All right. I'll go up to a million. One million dollars for three months. After that, you can file for a divorce."

My hand flies in the air, taking the gift bag with it. I narrowly miss crashing it into the side of Mr. Locke's head. "Slow this crazy train down."

"One and a half million, Miss Shaw." He scrubs the back of his neck. "You drive a hard bargain."

I've said all of seven words during this negotiation. That's not driving a hard bargain. That's bewilderment.

Cursing under his breath, he whips his phone from his jacket pocket.

What the hell is happening now?

His fingers dance over the screen before he turns his back on me.

It's a futile move since I can hear every word that comes out of his mouth.

"Judge?" he says before he takes a pause. "We're running behind. Can you marry us in your chambers this evening?"

I tap him on the shoulder. "Tonight won't work for me."

He spins around. His blue eyes rake me from head to toe. I can't tell if that's his signature '*What the fuck?*' look or if he wants to fuck me.

I chase that thought away because where did it come from?

"We'll see you then," he says to the judge.

He pockets the phone before he gives me his full attention again. "I'll have my attorney write up an amendment to the prenuptial agreement to include the one and a half million payable on the day you file for a divorce."

He reaches into the inner pocket of his jacket to show me the corner of a white envelope.

"You have a prenup with you?" I ask with a chuckle. "You're kidding, right?"

He taps the face of his watch with his index finger. "We have thirty minutes to get the marriage license, Miss Shaw. At the very least, agree to that. We can work out the other details between now and when we see the judge."

I see something in his eyes that I've never seen before. It may be a plea, or it could be frustration, but against all of my better judgment and the nagging voice in the back of my head telling me to turn and walk away, I nod. "Just the license. Then we'll talk."

CHAPTER FIVE

Trina

I STARE at the marriage license in my lap that bears not only my name but my boss's name too.

How is any of this real?

When we went into the City Clerk's office, Mr. Locke's lawyer was waiting for us. Apparently, he was going to be the witness to our wedding.

He introduced himself as Morty no last name.

That's exactly what he said. "I'm Morty." Then he paused and added with a wink, "No last name."

He laughed like it was the funniest thing he'd ever heard.

I didn't break a grin because his attempt at a joke only added to my trepidation.

Still, I handed over my driver's license to the clerk behind the counter, signed on the dotted line, and in theory agreed to be my boss's wife.

It's not official until we go before the judge. That doesn't happen for another fifty-nine minutes, according to my watch.

I turn when I hear Mr. Locke enter his office behind me. I sat down on one of the visitor chairs that face his desk while he and Morty No-Last-Name had a hushed discussion next to my desk.

All I heard was Morty saying that he had to get home before seven and Mr. Locke calling someone who works for the judge to ask if they would witness his wedding.

His wedding. Not our wedding.

If that isn't a red flag waving in the breeze right over my head, I don't know what is.

I should pop open the bottle of champagne in the gift bag on the corner of Mr. Locke's desk, race out of here, and celebrate being a single woman in the big city.

Instead, I'm sitting here trying to find the right words to let my boss down easily. Honestly, I just want to walk out of here with a job, or at the very least, a stellar recommendation.

"Miss Shaw," Mr. Locke says my name in a rush. "The prenuptial agreement is ready for your perusal."

He drops a stack of papers on top of the wedding license.

"We added a few amendments in ink, and I initialed those." He points at the papers. "I assure you that it's all legal."

I take *no reassurance* in that.

I don't need to worry about that, because this wedding is not happening. "I'm not marrying you, sir."

He runs a finger under his bottom lip. "I assumed we were past the question of whether or not this was happening."

"We weren't," I state with a shake of my head. "I can't marry you."

"You can."

Marriage means something to me. I've watched my

parents navigate the waters of a successful marriage. I want that too.

"I believe one and a half million dollars is more than generous, Miss Shaw."

It's ridiculous.

I've yet to hit the six-figure a year mark for my annual salary. One and a half million dollars would secure my financial future, but it comes at a cost that's too steep.

"It's very generous," I agree. "But when I get married, I want it to be for love, and I want the first time to be the only time."

Leaning against the edge of his desk, he crosses his arms. "We'll be divorced a few months from now. After that, you're free and clear to marry a man you love."

I scratch my head. "You keep bringing up divorce. An annulment is an option."

I can't believe I'm even considering this arrangement, but on the remote chance that I do it, I don't want there to be any public record that I married this man.

"That's not an option."

"It is," I insist. "People get annulments all the time."

I'm basing that on what I've seen in the movies and on television.

"It's not an option," he repeats.

Frustrated, I inch forward on my chair. "I happen to know that if a marriage is never consummated, it can be annulled, and since we will never do that, it's an option."

Mr. Locke's fingers trace his jaw. "In New York State, that's only an option if one party is physically unable to have sex. I sure as hell don't fall into that category, Miss Shaw, do you?"

How am I talking about sex with my boss right now?

I can't form a verbal response, so I shake my head.

"Divorce is the route we'll take," he says matter-of-factly. "If it helps, remind yourself that this is strictly for convenience, and when you do marry for love, it will be for the first time."

Technically he's right, but I'll always know I said *I do* to my boss to pad my bank account. I have to live with that, and I'm not sure I can regardless of how much money he's offering me.

"I don't understand why you told Mr. Abdon we were married in the first place," I say with a hint of exasperation in my tone. "How did that happen?"

He closes his eyes briefly and draws a deep breath.

"It's easy to tell him that we're not married," I go on, "I can do it if you'd prefer."

I wouldn't say I have a friendship with Lloyd Abdon, but I know he's fond of me. He's told me that every time he's come into the office.

Mr. Locke studies my face. "Lloyd told me I was fucking up my life."

My eyes widen. "What?"

He tilts his head back. "We discussed my future plans outside of the office, and I didn't have an answer that fits into what he considers acceptable."

That's a lot of words that say very little, so I ask for clarification. "I don't understand."

"Since he promoted me to CEO, he's asked about the women in my life." He glances toward the open doorway of his office. "There hasn't been anyone worth discussing, so he started bringing you up."

"Me?" I ask, feeling a blush creep up my cheeks.

"Miss Shaw is a remarkable person." He taps a finger against his palm. "Miss Shaw is smart and kind. She's a considerate young woman."

"Mr. Abdon said those things about me?"

"And more." He nods. "Eventually, I told him we were seeing each other outside the office. I thought that would be enough to appease him, but he kept pressing me to pop the question and set a date, so I told him the other day we were married in a civil ceremony this week. The words came out before I could stop myself."

I've known Mr. Locke for more than a year, and I'd never peg him as someone who bows to pressure, not even pressure applied at the hand of his boss.

"Lloyd has relocated to Paris, so I assumed he'd stay there." He scrubs a hand over the back of his neck. "This visit was unexpected."

He has filled in some of the blanks, but I still feel I'm missing a big piece of this puzzle.

I try a new approach. "You said that I could file for a divorce ninety days from now."

"That's right."

"Why ninety days?" I ask with a perk of my brow. "Are you going to tell Mr. Abdon that I left you three months into our marriage because of your attitude?"

A smirk settles over his lips. "My attitude?"

I nod.

I'm not giving him more than that because I really need that letter of recommendation. The chances of me walking out of here with a job are looking less likely by the second.

"Three months is sufficient," he says.

That's all he says.

It's as though the rest of his explanation just fell off the edge of a cliff and is forever lost in the abyss of confusion that is my life right now.

"Sufficient?" I repeat. "Explain that, please, sir."

He glances down at his watch. He knows that the minutes are ticking away.

"Sir?" I wave my hand in the air to get his attention. "What did you mean when you said that three months is sufficient?"

Before I can move my hand, he has it wrapped in his.

It's the first time I've ever touched Graham Locke. We didn't shake hands when we met, and he's always been mindful of my personal space.

His eyes find mine. "Miss Shaw."

"Yes?" I reply in a soft tone.

"Mr. Abdon is ill." He swallows hard. "He told me that he has limited time left. He wants to spend the next two to three months in New York City tying up loose ends with the business. Then he plans on returning to Paris to live his final days. You'll need to stay married to me until he's back in France or God forbid if he doesn't make it back, until he…"

I draw in a quick breath. "He's sick?"

"He doesn't want anyone to know." He squeezes my hand. "I made a promise to him that I'd keep that between the two of us."

Tears threaten, but I blink them back, determined to keep a sound mind during this discussion.

"Mr. Abdon has no family to speak of," he goes on. "This marriage that he believes has taken place means a great deal to him."

This changes everything. Mr. Abdon is a good person.

I met him when I was in the lobby of this building. I walked into the wrong skyscraper on my way to a job interview. I asked Mr. Abdon to help direct me to the right place, not realizing who he was.

He asked to see a copy of my resume. I showed him the

one in my purse, and he hired me on the spot to be the assistant to the CEO.

My gaze drops to the prenup.

If I can help keep a smile on Mr. Abdon's face while he's in Manhattan, that's worth more than any amount of money my boss is offering. I admit the money won't go to waste, though.

"Deceiving him when he was across an ocean was hard enough," he confesses. "I can't look him in the eye and tell him we're married if we're not. I need this to happen, Miss Shaw. He's the best person I've ever known. I want his final days to be happy."

"I'll marry you," I whisper. "But I'm only doing it for Mr. Abdon."

"That's the only reason I'm marrying you," my future husband says. "Sign on the dotted line, Miss Shaw, and let's get to the courthouse."

CHAPTER SIX

Graham

JESUS. What a goddamn day this is turning out to be.

I was moving through the trials and tribulations of any typical weekday when my boss tossed me a curveball that upended my entire life. I didn't foresee Lloyd Abdon making a last minute trip to Manhattan, but it's happening.

I'm standing in front of Judge Peggy Mycella with my assistant by my side as we exchange vows.

"I do," I blurt out, likely before I was prompted to.

Miss Shaw glances at me with some serious side-eye.

Peggy sighs. "Graham, it wasn't your turn. I was asking Trina if she takes you to be her lawfully wedded husband."

"I don't have a choice," Miss Shaw answers.

That drives Peggy's gaze in her direction. "You always have a choice, Trina."

My assistant shakes her head. "My choice is to do the right thing, so I have to do it. I have to marry him."

"Are you pregnant?" Peggy asks. "I realize that asking

that question is outside of the boundary of everything that is appropriate, but I know firsthand that a capable woman can raise a child on her own. Besides, Graham may be far from perfect, but given his past, I trust that he would step up and help monetarily and in other ways with his child."

What the fuck?

"Pregnant?" Miss Shaw's mouth drops open. "We've never had sex."

Peggy's eyes widen as her gaze shifts back to me. "That's surprising, but I respect it. Waiting until you're married will make your first time together that much more special."

For Christ's sake. I just want this ceremony to be over.

"She does," I state calmly. "Miss Shaw does take me to be her husband."

Peggy sighs heavily. "Perhaps we should take a moment to discuss this. I'm wondering if Trina is invested in this as deeply as you are, Graham."

"I do," Miss Shaw says. "I'll do it. Yes. I'll marry him."

That's one hurdle behind me.

I roll my hand in the air. "Get to my part."

Peggy slides her glasses back up the bridge of her nose and drops her gaze to the paper in her hand. "Graham Locke, do you take this woman to be your lawfully wedded wife? Do you promise to love and honor her, and…"

"I do," I shout. "I'll do it all."

That lures a smile from Peggy. "I love seeing that kind of exuberance from a groom. I suppose you're in a hurry to get this over with so you can start on the wedding night festivities."

"Sure," I say just as Miss Shaw drops a muted, "no way" from her lips.

I yank the ring box I tried to give my almost wife earlier

out of my jacket pocket. I pop open the lid. "Let's get to the rings."

Peggy bends down to look at the stunning five-carat diamond ring I bought a few hours ago. "Oh, my word, that is a ring."

It was the store clerk's choice. She went on about how any woman would be forever grateful to wear this ring. I rushed her along by waving my credit card in her face after telling her to pick a wedding band for me. Once we found one that fit, I paid and took off with both rings.

I dive my hand back into my pocket to retrieve the plain silver band that will adorn my ring finger for the next ninety days.

We go through the task of sliding rings on each other's fingers before we turn to face Peggy one last time.

"By the power vested in me by the State of New York, I now pronounce you husband and wife," she pauses. "You may now kiss your bride, Graham."

I turn to Miss Shaw.

Wanting to avoid any further questions from Peggy, I intend to close out this show with a memorable kiss.

My wife has other plans.

She plants a hand on my shoulder, leans closer, and touches her lips to my cheek.

THE FIRST THING I noticed about Miss Shaw when I met her was how unbelievably beautiful she is.

She's tall. I'm six feet, and when she's in heels, as she is now, we're nose to nose.

Her blue eyes are strikingly vibrant. They are mesmerizing to the point that it's distracting. Her hair is golden blonde, and when she doesn't pin it up, it cascades around her shoulders.

When Lloyd announced that she was my new assistant, I panicked briefly. If I had bumped into her in the lobby that day instead of him, I would have asked her out and likely pursued her until I had her in bed.

Since I've gotten to know her, I've realized that we're far too different to connect on any level other than one that aligns us as allies in the office.

Yet, here we are.

Married temporarily, and it's all because of my reckless pursuit to please a man who gave me a chance when no one else would.

I owe Lloyd Abdon far more than I can ever repay him for.

I only hope what I did today will give him some sense of joy.

"Can I go home now?" Miss Shaw asks as we exit the courthouse.

I didn't think this plan through to the point of living arrangements, but since Lloyd isn't set to step on a plane bound for New York for a few more hours, I nod. "Of course."

Her gaze drops to the diamond ring on her finger. "You went all out on this. I'll take good care of it until we're divorced."

"It's yours to keep, Miss Shaw."

Her eyes meet mine. "I don't want to keep it."

"You will," I say simply. "I have a prior engagement, so I'll call a car to see you home safely."

"A prior engagement?" Her tone suggests the question dives deeper than surface level.

I'm not going to discuss my romantic past with my wife. There was no prior engagement or anything serious at all.

There was work and a few short-term relationships to fill my time until I found more work to do.

I'm twenty-nine. Marriage wasn't something I even vaguely considered before this morning.

"Yes," I answer.

She doesn't press for more, and I don't offer anything beyond that one word reply. There's no need to tell her that I'm meeting my three closest friends for dinner.

I tug my phone from the inner pocket of my jacket with the intention of calling one of our company drivers to pick up Miss Shaw.

Her hand moves to my forearm. "I can get home on my own, sir."

I glance at her. "Graham. Please try and call me Graham when we're in the presence of Mr. Abdon."

"Graham," she repeats.

I nod.

"I'm going to take the subway," she says as she twirls the ring on her finger to hide the diamond from view. "I'll see you at the office tomorrow."

"Goodnight, Miss Shaw."

Her lips lift into a soft smile. "It's Trina or Mrs. Locke."

Indeed it is.

"Trina, " I go for the less jarring choice. "Goodnight, Trina."

"Bye, Graham." She wiggles her fingers in the air before she starts in a brisk walk down the sidewalk.

CHAPTER SEVEN

Trina

I STARE at the ring on my finger.

I half-convinced myself before I fell asleep last night that I'd wake this morning to realize that it was all a dream, but this stunning diamond ring says otherwise.

Even though I'm not changing my name legally for this temporary arrangement, Mr. Abdon will still view me as Trina Locke.

"Trina Locke," I whisper. "Mrs. Locke."

When I blurted it out to Mr. Locke last night, it was a joke. Now, I'm starting to realize just how uncomfortable it makes me to say it and hear it.

I finish brushing my hair before dressing in a navy blue pencil skirt and a light blue blouse.

Blue is my color.

I've had enough people tell me that to convince me it's true.

Just as I'm about to slip my feet into a pair of nude heels, my phone chimes from my bedside table.

I rush over and pick it up to read the text message on the screen.

> ***Mr. Locke:*** **Mr. Abdon will be arriving in New York shortly after 1 PM. I'll forward you his itinerary. Schedule a car to pick him up from the airport and make arrangements for his stay at the Bishop Hotel Tribeca.**

NO GOOD MORNING, or how are you doing, wife… nothing but another one of his curt orders.

This one is different, though, and I intend to treat it as such.

I type back a response.

> ***Trina:*** **I'll handle it.**

ONCE I HIT SEND, I open my contact list and scroll down to my boss's name. I edit the details switching out Mr. Locke for Graham.

If I'm going to train my brain to call him that, I need to start this very second.

Another text message arrives just as I go back to the messaging app.

> *Graham:* **As you're aware, I'll be in meetings most of the day. I suggest we discuss what to say to Lloyd before we meet him at the hotel later for a drink. Agreed?**

YEAH, no.

I won't agree to that.

I'm not sending one of the company's drivers to the airport to pick up its founder. That will not happen on my watch.

I choose my words carefully before I text Graham back.

> *Trina:* **You have an opening at 4. I'll be at my desk.**

I PRESS SEND, leave my bedroom, and head to the kitchen for a quick breakfast before I start my first official day as Mrs. Locke.

―――

WORRY SETTLES in my belly as I watch the passengers that were on the same flight as Mr. Abdon file past me.

I'm at JFK airport waiting in the arrival area for Mr. Abdon.

I know, for sure, that he would have deplaned first. He always deplanes first because he's superstitious about where he will sit on an airplane.

"It's the first row all the way, Trina," he told me once.

I remembered that advice on the day I took my first flight ever. I was headed to Cincinnati to visit my sister, Falon, and her husband, Asher Foster.

The trip was their gift for my twenty-fourth birthday, including the first class airline ticket.

I sat in the second row that day, terrified and excited at the same time. When the plane landed, Falon was there to greet me. She took me to the hotel they were staying in and checked me into a luxury suite. A few hours later, we watched her husband perform to a sold-out crowd on the final stop of his world tour.

My brother-in-law just happens to be a rock star.

He offered me a job when I graduated from college. I jumped at the chance to handle the duties of being his assistant, but over time, I realized that mixing business with family wasn't for me.

I had to venture out on my own, and fortunately for me, Mr. Abdon fell into my path.

I breathe a sigh of relief when he appears.

I can tell immediately that he's changed since the last time I saw him months ago. He's thinner, he's walking more slowly, and the usual bounce in his gait isn't there anymore.

Rushing toward him, I hold up the makeshift sign I made before I left the office.

His laughter fills the terminal once he spots it and me.

"World's most handsome watchmaker," he reads it aloud. "If that's not fuel for my weary soul, I don't know what is."

Before I can say anything, he tugs me into an embrace.

It's the first time he's done that, and I relish in it. I hold him tightly as he clings to me.

"Oh no," he whispers close to my ear. "I'm in trouble."

Fear darts through me as I step back. I search his face for a clue, worried that he's in medical distress. "Are you all right, sir?"

"Your husband is headed this way." He tilts his chin up. "And he doesn't look happy."

It takes me a second to unpack that because I've only had a husband for less than a day.

I turn to see Graham walking toward us.

Well, hello, hot husband.

The man is turning heads. He's looking all kinds of perfect in his gray suit. His hair is slightly messy, which is a new look for him. I like it. I like it a lot.

He darts a hand through it as though he can read my mind. "It's windy outside."

My eyes catch on the silver band on his left hand.

I put that there. It may be temporary and have little meaning, but my heart doesn't get that memo because it starts pounding inside my chest.

"Trina," he says my name quietly. "I didn't expect you to be here. I thought you were busy."

"I rearranged my schedule, Graham." I turn to look at Mr. Abdon when I hear the tremor in my voice. "I couldn't miss the opportunity to welcome Mr. Abdon home."

"Lloyd," Mr. Abdon insists as he reaches for my hand. "It's time you start calling me Lloyd."

He winks the same way he always does whenever he sneaks the words *time* or *watch* into a sentence.

Graham moves to grab hold of Lloyd's forearm. I can tell that his touch is soft as he leads the older man forward by a step. "Let's get you to the hotel."

"Hotel?" Lloyd's gaze volleys between Graham and me. "I happen to know that penthouse you live in has a handful of bedrooms. I assumed I'd be staying with the newlyweds, or is that overstepping?"

Graham's eyes lock on mine.

I stare at him in disbelief. I'm all for pretending to be his wife in name only, but the solace in that is at the end of the day, I can go home, kick off my shoes, take off my bra, and be Trina Shaw again.

Without blinking, my husband answers, "I wouldn't have it any other way, Lloyd. Trina and I would love to have you as our houseguest."

CHAPTER EIGHT

Graham

I'VE BEEN MARRIED for less than a day, and I'm reasonably sure that my wife is plotting my murder.

She hasn't so much as glanced in my direction since I invited Lloyd to stay with me or us.

We are in the lobby of my building now as Trina takes it all in.

I wish to hell she didn't look so surprised by the elegant décor and grand entrance to the building.

Thankfully, Lloyd hasn't noticed that my bride is stunned into silence since this is her first time seeing what is supposed to be her home sweet home.

"I'll need to rest once we're upstairs, " Lloyd announces, and I almost reach over to plant a kiss in the middle of his forehead to thank him.

I'm going to use that time wisely to convince my assistant to move in with me.

His proclamation stops Trina mid-step. She glances at me.

"In that case, I think I'll head back to the office. There are some things I need to take care of."

If one of those things is to file for a divorce, I'm in a hell of a lot of trouble.

I paste a forced grin on my face as we walk on either side of Lloyd on our way toward the bank of elevators. "Let's get Lloyd settled in the guest room in the east wing before you do that."

"East wing?" she mouths to herself.

I catch the look of disbelief on her face.

The penthouse was a sound investment during a time I was looking for a place to settle down. The fact that it has six bedrooms, a sauna, a rooftop terrace, and a killer view are all bonuses.

My plan has always been to sell in several years to pocket the profit, as the area is experiencing a steady uptick in property values.

"That's my favorite room," Lloyd mutters as I guide him onto the elevator. "It's near the library."

Trina tosses me a look that makes me wonder if she thinks I'm illiterate.

The library is a room that I've yet to step foot in. The previous owner left behind the books that line the shelves, or rather her attorney did. Her death made the news because of her philanthropy and the fact that she had no family to speak of.

I share that in common with the dearly departed. Family is only a word to me since I don't have one.

I tap my keycard against the elevator panel to light up the button marked P1.

Penthouse 1.

It's misleading, as there is only one Penthouse on the property. The remaining apartments are all impressive in their own right, but they don't require a keycard to access the button that leads to their floors.

"I know Graham can't boil water but do you cook, Trina?"

Lloyd's question draws my assistant's gaze to me before it settles on my boss. "I'm a great cook."

That doesn't surprise me.

I've learned that Trina Shaw is skilled in many things, including managing me.

Her ability to handle everything I toss in her direction is impressive.

"Would you consider…"

"Cooking for you?" Trina interrupts Lloyd before he can finish his thought. "I would love to do that, sir."

That will require food, which is something I don't have in abundance in my home, or have at all.

"Do you have any special requests?" Her beautiful blue eyes light up as she asks the question.

Lloyd's a goner. I see it in his expression as he gazes at my wife. "Why don't you surprise me?"

Trina glances at me. "I'll pick up what I need to cook something fabulous on my way back here from the office."

Knowing that she's talking about my penthouse, I gaze at the floor. Not only will we need food, but we'll also need whatever is required to cook a meal. Pots? Pans? A spatula?

The elevator dings its arrival on my floor. When the doors slide open, Lloyd steps out and into the foyer of my penthouse. I follow.

Trina remains in place.

I urge her forward with a curl of my finger.

Lloyd's back is to her, so she shakes her head adamantly as panic flashes over her expression.

Once Lloyd is past me, I take a step closer to my wife,

extend a hand, and manage a smile. "Let's get our guest settled in. Then we can have a moment alone."

"Newlyweds," Lloyd quips as he turns to face us. "You two remind me of my sweet darling and me right after we married."

I feel the tremor of Trina's hand at the mention of Lloyd's late wife.

I squeeze it to reassure her as I lead her off the elevator and into my home.

CHAPTER NINE

Trina

THIS SITUATION HAS GONE from bad to *holy-heck-what-have-I-gotten-myself-into* in record time.

Not only do I need to keep up the façade of being Mr. Locke's wife, but I have to play the part on a full-time basis.

I don't know if I have the acting chops to pull off this charade.

I follow Graham and Lloyd down a series of twisting hallways until we reach double doors. Graham opens them, and I'm greeted with the sight of a spacious bedroom decorated in earthy tones.

The view through the windows is quintessential New York City. Many of the most recognizable buildings in Manhattan dot the skyline.

If this is the guestroom, I can't begin to imagine what Mr. Locke's bedroom looks like.

Panic drops over me.

Is his bedroom now my bedroom?

I didn't sign up to share that intimate of a space with my boss.

Surely, given how ridiculously spacious this property is, there's a bedroom tucked away somewhere that I can use.

Lloyd glances over his shoulder. "You must admit that this is one of your very favorite rooms in the penthouse."

I've only seen the main living area and the never-ending hallways that brought us here, so I nod. "It's something else."

It's unnecessary.

No one needs this much glitz and glamour when they are sleeping.

There's a fireplace on the wall that separates the bedroom from the bathroom. The floors are redwood, and the artwork that decorates the space is expensive. I know. I've seen a Brighton Beck original hanging in Falon's apartment, and if I'm not mistaken, I'm staring at another one of his watercolor paintings hung over the bed.

Graham places Mr. Abdon's suitcase on a luggage rack in the corner near a brown leather chair.

He unzips it but doesn't take the next step of opening it.

"We'll leave you to rest, Lloyd." Graham points at a phone on the bedside table. "Dial zero if you need anything. It will ring straight through to my cell."

That's a fancy set-up. I could use that in my apartment if I didn't live alone and the kitchen wasn't ten feet from my bedroom.

Lloyd turns to face me. "I'm looking forward to spending time with both of you, Trina. I'm grateful that you've allowed me the honor of staying in your home."

I stay silent because this isn't my home.

"Our home is your home," Graham interjects. "Rest well, Lloyd. We'll wake you in a few hours."

"FOLLOW ME," my husband says as soon as he closes the doors to the guestroom.

I fall in step behind him as we wander down the series of hallways until we are back in the main living area.

This room is just as over-the-top as the guest bedroom. Chocolate brown leather furniture sits atop an exquisite rug. The flooring below is a shade lighter than in the guest bedroom, and the fireplace is beautiful white stone with a large wooden mantle.

"This way," Graham says as he jerks a thumb toward another hallway. "We're going to the kitchen."

I can't wait to see that.

When we round the corner, and my gaze settles on the white cabinetry, large island, and flawless granite countertops, I almost salivate.

This is gorgeous with a capital G.

"Trina," Graham huffs out my name. "This is fucked up."

I tear my gaze away from the custom range hood to look at him. "It's very fucked up."

He almost smiles. "You need to stay here for the duration of Lloyd's trip."

"Why can't I sneak out at night and come back in the morning?" I ask, thinking that it's a solid plan.

My boss studies me. "You'll be comfortable here."

That's a non-answer to my very serious question, so I rephrase. "I'll go home after Lloyd goes to bed, and it won't take me long to get back here in the mornings. I'll have breakfast ready and waiting by the time he wakes up every day."

"There are too many variables for that to be a viable option."

That's a wordy way of shooting my idea down, so I press forward. "What variables?"

Graham leans his hip against the kitchen island. "You could oversleep. He could wake up early. What happens if he becomes ill during the night and I have to call 9-1-1? You don't think he'd wonder why you're not around?"

My eyes widen. "Is that a possibility? Is there a chance that he may need to be hospitalized during this trip?"

"Anything is possible."

I shake my head. "I'm not sleeping in the same room as you."

"God, no." He chuckles. "You'll take my bedroom. I'll stay in the adjoining room with the door between closed unless there is an emergency."

"There's a bedroom that hooks up with your bedroom?" I ask in disbelief.

His eyes search my face. "It's the smallest bedroom. I sense it was designed to be a nursery."

"Oh," I say, caught off guard. "I suppose that could work."

"It will work," he counters matter-of-factly. "I'll send someone to gather your belongings if that's easier for you."

I grew up with twelve siblings. I don't need anyone touching my stuff. That's one of the reasons I live alone now.

"I'll go home and pack a suitcase."

"All right." His arms cross his chest. "Let's discuss dinner."

I glance around the kitchen again. "I have a lot to work with here. This is impressive, Mr. Locke."

"Graham," he stresses. "It's a showpiece, Trina. Other than a coffee machine and a few mismatched glasses, dishes, and utensils, it's barren."

To prove the point, he opens an upper cabinet door to

show me that it's empty. He yanks on a drawer pull too, and I spot nothing inside.

"I'll need a list of everything you require to cook a meal for Lloyd."

As overwhelming as that sounds, I nod. "My sister, Ida, works at a kitchen supply store. I can call her and ask her to send over everything I need."

He shoots me a look. "Does your sister know that we're married?"

I fist my hands together. "No, and I want to keep it that way. I'll tell her that you just moved in and are looking for all the essentials."

"That works for me."

"What about food?" I ask with a wince. "What do you have to work with?"

"Coffee and sugar."

"And?"

"Bottled water and wine," he adds. "I don't cook, Trina. I eat out. I always eat out."

Eat out.

The sound of those two words falling from his lips sends a charge through me even though he's clearly talking about take-out and not taking me to his bed.

It's just my luck that I'm married to the sexiest man I've ever met, and we'll never touch each other.

"If you make a list of everything you need, I'll have it all delivered."

I sigh. "I'll get started on that. I can email it to you when I'm done."

"And you'll head to your home now to pack?" he asks quietly. "If you need help, I can arrange for someone to stop by."

I don't bother asking who since I can handle it on my own. "I'll be fine."

"I'm going to work from home for the remainder of the day." He loosens his tie. "I'll be in my study. Please stop in when you get back."

"All right," I say, even though I have no clue which hallway maze would take me to the study.

"I'll see you out." His hand disappears into the inner pocket of his suit jacket. He yanks out the keycard he used earlier. "Use this when you get back."

I take it from him. "Thank you, sir."

"Graham," he reminds me with a smirk on his lips. "Your husband, remember?"

How the hell could I forget?

CHAPTER TEN

TRINA

I SIT on the edge of my bed and finish off the list of groceries for Graham. I read the email again to make sure I haven't missed anything and then finally press send.

I compiled the list while I was talking to my sister, Ida, on speakerphone. She had a few questions about why my boss needs an entire kitchen stocked with pots, pans, and every bell and whistle imaginable.

I went with the easy answer and told her that he recently moved into a new home and is looking for a fresh start.

Turning, I survey my bedroom and the small closet that holds all of my clothes.

My suitcase is tucked in the corner of it. I've only ever used it once, and that was during the trip to Cincinnati.

I start toward the closet, but a knock on my apartment door stops me in place.

Panicking, I glance down at the diamond ring on my left hand.

If a member of my family is standing on the other side of the door, I'll have a lot of explaining to do. I'm hoping that I can get through the next ninety days without any of them finding out that I married Graham.

I won't hold back the fact forever, but I will wait to tell them until I've filed for divorce.

If I don't, I'll have to deal with my parents' disappointment and a never-ending stream of questions from my siblings.

I slide the ring from my finger and place it carefully on my nightstand next to the base of a lamp.

Then I smooth my hands over the front of my skirt, take a deep breath and head straight for the door.

I swing it open without bothering to peer through the peephole.

I smile when I see who is standing there.

"Aurora." I glance down the hallway to her closed apartment door. "To what do I owe this mid-day visit?"

She tries to peer around me. "Is everything all right, Trina?"

No. I'm married to my boss, and I have to go camp out at his place to play make-believe for who knows how long.

I hold that in because the situation is as absurd as it sounds.

"Just taking a break." I lean against the doorjamb. "How are you? How's Eldon?"

"Good and good."

I wait for more, but she's still focused on what's behind me. If memory serves me correctly, it's nothing special. The only thing in her line of sight worth looking at is the one houseplant that I've managed to keep alive for the past four months.

I suddenly realize that the plant will likely outlast my first marriage.

"Are you working today?" I ask to fill in the silence.

She shakes her head. "I have the day off. I heard your door slam shut, so I wanted to be sure everything was okay."

"All is great in my world," I lie.

She grins. "You should drop by the café for a coffee one day soon."

"I'd love that," I say honestly.

I need that.

I miss hanging out with her.

"I'll text you my work schedule so you know when to stop by." She pats the back pocket of her jeans where her phone always is. "I think I'll go for a walk. Are you going back to the office now?"

I wish.

"I have a couple of things to do before I take off." I glance down at my watch. "We'll talk soon?"

"You know it." She tugs me into an unexpected embrace. "I'm glad I knocked on your door. It's good to see you."

I step back to study her. "Is everything okay, Aurora?"

"It is." She raises her hand in the air. "I swear."

I can tell she could use a friend, but my time is limited. I don't know when Lloyd will wake up, but I want to be there for that and for the delivery that Ida is sending to Graham's home.

"I should be the one asking you that." She smiles. "You look stressed. Is your boss being an asshole again?"

"Something like that," I mutter.

"Look on the bright side."

"What's the bright side?" I wrinkle my nose.

"At least you're not married to the guy."

How I wish that were still true. In the past twenty-four

hours, I've not only married the guy, but I've also become so deeply entangled in his life that I'm going to be living under the same roof as him.

"You're supposed to agree with me," Aurora says through a stilted giggle. "Unless you secretly want to marry him."

Feeling cornered, I bark out a laugh. "Oh, Aurora."

"I know, I know." She sighs. "From what you've told me, he's a heartless bastard who doesn't have a compassionate bone in his body. I know you well enough to know that you'd never marry someone like that."

But, I did, and within the hour, I'll be moving into his home with the hope that I'll come out of this marriage as the same woman I am today.

CHAPTER ELEVEN

Trina

WHEN THE ELEVATOR doors slide open to reveal the foyer to Graham's apartment, I shove the keycard in the back pocket of my jeans.

I changed clothes before I came over since I realized that I wasn't going back to the office today.

My official workday is done, but this show that Graham and I are putting on for Mr. Abdon is just getting started.

I glance up to see something even more breathtaking than the penthouse.

My boss is standing to the left dressed in faded jeans and a black T-shirt. That's giving me an unobstructed view of his muscular arms. His left forearm has a black and gray tattoo wrapped around it, but if I stare any harder, he's going to take notice.

Who knew he was even more gorgeous dressed down?

"Trina." My name snaps from his lips. "You made it."

As if I had a choice.

It's not just the one and half million dollars that dragged my ass and most of my clothing here, but it's Mr. Abdon.

I don't want to let him down.

Graham stalks toward me to grab the handle of my overstuffed suitcase. He picks it up with ease. "I'll put this in my bedroom."

I don't wait for an invitation to follow him. I do it because I need to know the route when this day is finally over.

It's a much less complicated path to his bedroom than it is to the guest one.

Once again, large wooden double doors await us.

"If this isn't up to your standards, there are several other bedrooms." He tosses me a look. "I expect you to let me know if you're comfortable."

Feeling as though I'm about to enter a palace, I smile. "I'll be fine here, sir."

He cocks a brow.

"Graham," I correct myself. "I meant Graham."

He turns one of the door handles and steps aside. "After you."

I hold in my surprise as I enter his bedroom. This is not at all what I was expecting.

It's much smaller than the guest room. A king size bed takes up most of the space. The view beyond the window is of the side of a building next door. It's the only building on the block that's taller than this one.

There is no fireplace or expensive artwork on the walls, but the ambiance is welcoming. It's cozy, and the colors on the curtains on the window and the bedding are shades of gray with accents of black and white.

Graham steps around me to place my suitcase on the floor near the foot of the bed. "As I said, if it's not suitable, I can relocate you to another room."

I glance at him. "It's fine. I like it."

His finger juts out to point to two closed doors. "There's a bathroom to the left, and the walk-in closet is empty. I moved my things into the adjoining room."

That tracks my gaze to the right and an open doorway. "That's over there?"

He nods. "Yes. We'll keep that door closed unless there's a reason for me to join you in here."

Our eyes meet for the briefest of moments.

Barring an emergency with Mr. Abdon, there should be absolutely no reason for Graham to join me in here.

Even though I kind of might want him to at some point.

I chase that thought away because he sure as hell doesn't think about me that way.

"I suspect we have another hour or two before Lloyd wakes up." He pinches the bridge of his nose. "Take some time to unpack, and then we'll get started in the kitchen."

"All right," I say quietly.

This is really happening. I'm temporarily moving in with my temporary husband.

Graham brushes past me on his way out of the room. Before he reaches the doorway, he turns back. "Thank you, Miss Shaw. This means a great deal to Lloyd."

I have to wonder if it means anything to him.

"I appreciate you putting your life on hold for the next ninety days." He drops his hands to his hips.

"Mr. Abdon gave me an incredible opportunity when he hired me. If I can do anything to make him happy, I want to."

His eyes bore into me as he studies me from head to toe. "He made the right decision that day, Trina."

Maybe. Maybe not.

Lloyd couldn't have known when he hired me that one

day I'd end up pretending to love, honor, and cherish his CEO.

"THAT WAS DELICIOUS, TRINA," Lloyd says as he wipes a linen napkin over his lips. "Chicken Piccata is a long time favorite of mine."

I breathe a sigh of relief. After arranging everything in Graham's kitchen, including putting away all of the groceries, I knew I had to whip up something quickly for dinner.

Chicken Piccata fit the bill. I paired it with a side salad and some crusty bread.

Graham chose a bottle of white wine, and by the time Lloyd woke from his nap, dinner was ready, and the dining room table was set.

I turn to him. "I'm glad you liked it."

My gaze wanders across the table to where Graham is seated. It was his choice to sit Lloyd at the head of the table with us on either side of him.

I had to struggle not to stare at my boss through dinner. I don't know what it is about him in his home, but it's captivating. Maybe it's because, for once, he looks somewhat relaxed and at ease.

I'm anything but since I'm still playing the role of Mrs. Locke with zero experience for inspiration.

"Trina." Mr. Abdon reaches for my left hand. "Let me see that."

I know he's talking about the ring because it's larger than life. I would have never chosen an engagement ring like this. I'm a firm believer that the size of the diamond doesn't measure the commitment.

I suppose, in this case, it doesn't matter what the ring looks like.

Lloyd draws my hand close to his face. "This is lovely."

I nod. I can't thank him for the compliment because the ring feels like a weight I can hardly bear right now.

I don't want to lie to the man who gave me a job without even checking my references. He trusted me that day. Now, I'm leading him down a path of dishonesty.

Lloyd suddenly drops my hand and pushes back from the table. "Will you excuse me for a minute? There's something in my room that I need."

Graham is on his feet before Lloyd is standing. "I'll get it for you."

"No." Lloyd pats a hand on Graham's shoulder. "Sit with your wife. Toast to your future and all the children you'll have. They'll fill this apartment with laughter and fun."

I down a big gulp of wine because that's way outside the realm of what I signed up for.

As soon as Lloyd disappears from view, Graham takes his seat. He raises his glass in the air. "To us and our future…"

"Don't say it," I warn with a wag of my finger in the air. "Marriage is one thing, but children are…"

Graham's laughter interrupts me. "If you could see the look on your face, Miss Shaw. It's priceless."

I can't hold back a grin as I touch my glass to the side of his. "To us making it through today."

With a nod, he takes a sip of wine. "The first of many to come."

CHAPTER TWELVE

Graham

THIS FEELS ODDLY *COMFORTABLE,* but that word itself feels surprisingly uncomfortable.

I've lived alone for the past eleven years.

Technically, it's eleven years and two months. I broke out on my own shortly after my eighteenth birthday. Since then, I've eaten most meals alone. I've spent many of my evenings at my office or in the study here.

The exceptions to that rule have been when I've been dating a woman, but the caveat to that is that I've never brought a woman home.

I've always readily agreed when I've been invited back to their apartments.

"What do you think Lloyd went to get?" Trina quizzes with a bounce of her blonde eyebrows.

I have no idea.

For all I know, he scurried away so he could give my wife and me some privacy. Not that we need it.

This is the first full day of this marriage, and although it's not as torturous as I imagined it to be, I'd rather be alone.

Solace is my soul mate.

That's been my motto for most of my life.

"His harmonica."

Trina's gaze narrows. "He plays the harmonica?"

I lean back in my chair. "Like a champ."

Her hand moves to brush her hair back from her forehead. It's an innocent move, but the light from the chandelier above reflects off of the diamond on her finger.

It's an unnecessary reminder that I'm legally tied to her for the time being.

"I hope he plays it for us," she says in an almost giddy tone.

"You're a fan, are you?"

She battles off a smile. "Who isn't?"

I raise a hand above my head.

"Seriously?" she asks with surprise edging her tone. "It takes talent to play any instrument and courage to do it in front of an audience."

"Says the woman who can play what instrument?"

A breathy sigh escapes her. "None. I'm not musically inclined."

I'm inclined to ask her to gift me with another one of those sighs because my dick took notice of that.

I'm not hard by any means, but I'm edging toward increased interest.

I've never seen my assistant in anything but business attire. Tonight, she's wearing ripped, faded jeans and a blue short sleeve sweater. It's snug, so the soft curve of her breasts catches my eye whenever I give in to the overwhelming urge to glance at her.

With her hair down in waves around her shoulders, she's stunning.

"What about you?" She tilts her head. "Can you play an instrument?"

I sip from my glass and then wait for a few seconds before I answer. "I play the piano."

"The piano?" That piques her interest enough that she leans forward to prop her elbows on the table. "You play the piano, or you mess around on the piano?"

"Mess around on the piano?" I repeat back. "I haven't tried that, but it's sturdy. I suppose it could withstand the impact."

It takes her a moment to unpack all of that. Her eyes wander over my face as she does, so I'm fortunate enough to catch the precise moment when she realizes that I'm talking about a *good hard fuck*.

"What did I miss?" Lloyd walks back into the room at the worst possible time.

"Nothing," Trina snaps. "We weren't talking about anything."

I hold in a laugh before turning my attention to him. I slide to my feet to help him get seated in his chair.

As I do that, he drops something in my palm.

Goddammit.

Every other curse word invented runs through my mind as I stare down at what he deposited in my hand.

"Trina." Lloyd turns his back on me so he can face my wife. "I noticed that you don't have a wedding band."

Trina's fingers trace over the large diamond on her left hand. "This is an engagement ring and a wedding band all in one."

It's a good comeback, but it's not going to stop what is about to happen.

Lloyd shakes his head. "The wedding band is the anchor. It anchors both the engagement ring and your heart in place. Without one, you're not bound forever to Graham, so I have something for you."

I fist my hand around the diamond-encrusted wedding band that Lloyd gave to me.

"What is it?" Trina whispers.

Lloyd glances up at me. "Give it to her, Graham. I put it on my precious Sela's finger many, many years ago. I want you to put it on Trina's now."

Panic darts over my wife's expression. "Oh no, we couldn't, sir. That's too special."

"Nonsense," he cuts her off. "Graham is going to put it on you. I have a feeling it will fit perfectly."

I see no way out of this, so I round the table and reach out a hand to my assistant.

She takes it tentatively before she allows me to help her to her feet.

"Say a few words," Lloyd instructs. "Let us know how much Trina means to you."

Well, shit.

I take her left hand in mine and slowly slide the band in place next to her engagement ring while I look into her striking blue eyes. "You've made one man very happy, Trina. It takes an extraordinary woman to make the commitment you've made to me."

Her gaze searches my face before it drops to the wedding band on her finger. When she glances back up, I see tears welling in the corners of her eyes.

"You must kiss the bride," Lloyd shouts. "Give me a replay of the wedding kiss."

Like hell I will.

I scoop a hand behind my wife's neck, drop the other to

her hip, and I take her mouth in a kiss that I want Lloyd to remember for as long as he lives.

CHAPTER THIRTEEN

TRINA

I WILL NEVER FORGET this kiss.

Who knew Mr. Locke had this in him?

The man knows how to leave a woman breathless. I'm proof of that.

I let my body guide me as my hands leap to his shoulders.

My lips part before he dives his tongue in for the briefest touch against mine.

It shouldn't leave me wanting more, but it does.

He breaks the kiss, and I instantly wish that I could transport back in time to that moment right before it happened so I could experience it again because that was the best first kiss in the history of first kisses.

We stare at each other as Lloyd claps.

He says something but the pounding beat of my heart echoes through me, drowning out everything else.

Graham steps back. "Trina will treasure the ring forever, Lloyd."

My gaze drops to the diamond band on my hand. Its meaning holds so much value that I can't look at it without tearing up. I take a deep breath and glance at Mr. Abdon to find him smiling broadly.

"I think Trina likes it as much as Sela did."

Guilt grips me from the inside out threatening a confession, but I swallow it back. I need to remember that this is what Mr. Abdon wants. We are fulfilling his dying wish, even if it feels utterly wrong in every possible way.

A noise sounds through the penthouse. It's an alarm of some sort. Graham and Lloyd don't look panicked, so I take my cue from them since I'm supposed to live here.

"Someone is here," Graham says nonchalantly.

What?

Someone is here? I didn't sign up to play the role of his wife for an audience larger than one. This show we are putting on is for Mr. Abdon only.

Graham tugs his phone out of the pocket of his pants. He glances down at the screen. "Dessert has arrived."

I was hoping that we'd skip right to bedtime after dinner.

This has been the second longest day of my life. Yesterday took top honors since I woke up single and ready to mingle and ended the day married to a man who doesn't know anything about me other than how exceptionally well I do my job.

"I can't wait." Lloyd rubs his palms together. "Tell me that you ordered Sela's favorite dessert of all time, Graham."

I hope to hell he did, or Mr. Abdon isn't going to be happy.

"I did," Graham reassures him with a pat on his shoulder. "I'll have the doorman bring it up. I think you're going to like it, Trina."

"Not as much as the kiss," Lloyd adds. "There's no denying how much you liked that, Trina."

I didn't think it was that obvious, but apparently, it was.

I sit myself back down while my husband heads toward the elevator.

Something tells me that this day is far from over. I'm going to need more wine to go with my dessert.

I NIBBLED my way through a piece of over-baked cheesecake topped with some sort of strawberry jelly masking as red syrup.

After his first bite, Mr. Abdon called it "*a wonderfully, decadent treat.*" If he genuinely thinks it is, I need to bring home a cheesecake from my family's bakery.

Not home. I don't live here. I'm staying here as part of the agreement I made with my boss.

I glance to where Mr. Abdon is running a fingertip over the last crumbs on his plate to scoop them up.

"Would you care for another piece, Lloyd?" Graham asks.

That would be his third, and while I still have no idea what medical issue he's battling, I can't imagine three pieces of cheesecake being what any doctor would order.

"Why don't we save what's left for tomorrow?" I stick my nose in the middle of their conversation. "I'll put it away."

I can do that now since Ida sent over an array of storage dishes in every size imaginable. I doubt Mr. Locke will use even one after our marriage ends. He'll go back to eating out.

"I like that idea." Lloyd pushes to his feet. "I think I'm going to call it a night."

Graham stands. "I'll see you to your room."

I get up from my chair too, but before I can say goodnight to Mr. Abdon, he's got his arms wrapped around me.

"Thank you for dinner, Trina." His voice cracks. "Thank you both for everything."

"You're welcome," I whisper, trying to keep my tone level even though emotions are racing through me.

"I'll see you in the morning," he says as he breaks our embrace. "I hope you and your hubby have a good night."

I have no idea what my husband is about to do with the rest of his night, but my plans involve a bubble bath, some Netflix, and a self pep talk focused on getting through tomorrow as my boss's wife.

"We will." Graham nods sagely.

I glance in his direction to find him staring at me.

I arch an eyebrow before I turn my attention back to Lloyd. "Goodnight, Mr. Abdon."

"Goodnight, Mrs. Locke." He winks. "I sure like the sound of that."

That makes one of us.

I can't wait until I can drop this lie, so that I can go back to my simple life as Trina Shaw.

CHAPTER FOURTEEN

Graham

"TRINA," I call out my assistant's name as soon as I notice something is out of place.

She glances in the direction of my office. "Yes, sir?"

I curl a finger to urge her toward me. "I need to speak with you in private."

Pushing back from her desk, she glances to the right and then to the left. "This is private."

She's right, of course.

I inherited this office from Lloyd when he decided to retire. It's tucked away from the other offices of the executives of the company. They have to tug open a heavy glass door, trudge down a long corridor, turn a corner and pass Miss Shaw before they have access to me.

No one, but the two of us, is present at the moment.

"Come in my office now, Miss Shaw."

She skims a palm over the front of the skirt she's wearing. If there's anything I can depend on day-to-day, it's that my assistant will always be wearing a plain blouse and a pencil skirt.

The color of the garments varies, as do the shoes she chooses to wear, but she sticks to the same script every day.

I'm not complaining.

I admired the red skirt and white blouse she has on in my kitchen this morning when I wandered in there after the aroma of freshly brewed coffee greeted me.

I found her settled on a stool next to the island with Lloyd by her side.

He was eating a bowl filled with what looked like oatmeal, fresh fruit, and some seeds sprinkled over the top of it.

There wasn't a portion waiting for me. I didn't expect there to be. Miss Shaw signed on as my wife, not my personal chef.

After she left for the office, I spent an hour with Lloyd before I promised him I'd stop at home mid-day to check on him.

Trina brushes past me as she enters my office.

I can't help but notice the soft scent of her perfume, or perhaps that's just her.

When the door clicks shut, she turns to face me.

I stay silent while she takes in the gray suit and light blue button-down shirt I'm wearing. I pride myself on looking impeccable every single day.

I'm the CEO of a globally recognized designer watch brand.

When Lloyd handed me the reins to the company, he reminded me that I'm the brand ambassador and to live my life accordingly.

I have, for the most part.

"What can I help you with?" My wife asks in a soft tone.

My cock hardens, as it has every fucking time I've been within ten feet of her since we were married two days ago.

I don't know if it's her voice, or her body, or a combination of that and the fact that she's effortlessly beautiful, but it's becoming increasingly harder to ignore my dick's reaction to her.

I look at her left hand. "Your rings, Trina. Where are they?"

That sends her gaze to my hands. "You're wearing your ring? Why?"

"Because we're married."

She gives her head a slight shake. "I'm aware."

I wait for her to expand on that, but she takes on the stance of a woman about to defend her position. Her feet part slightly as her hands fall to her hips.

This is in no way helping me in my battle to overcome this erection.

"You agreed to be my wife for three months," I remind her as I cross my arms over my chest. "If I wasn't clear, that was three months full-time. Twenty-four hours a day, Trina."

Her right hand darts to her left hand. I watch as she rubs her bare ring finger. "I see other people all day, sir. I don't want anyone who works here asking me who I married."

I considered that, along with every other possible complication.

"They are bound to find out."

"Why?" She sighs. "Aren't we doing all of this for Mr. Abdon's benefit only? Why drag anyone else into this farce?"

"Farce?" I fight back a chuckle.

"The word fits," she insists. "This is a farce. It's a sham. We are pulling the wool over Lloyd's eyes, and I, for one, feel shitty about it."

As do I, but I'd feel a whole lot shittier if I didn't grant him the wish of seeing me married to Miss Shaw before he dies.

"We are making him happy," I remind her.

Her eyes search my face. "I still feel guilty about it."

I'd admit the same, but I've learned that guilt can be viewed as a burden or an opportunity for real change. If you take that emotion and channel it into something useful, the weight of it lessens.

At least, that's what I tell myself.

"I haven't asked," she begins as she drops her gaze to the floor. "I haven't wanted to intrude, but I've been wondering about Mr. Abdon and his condition. What exactly is wrong with him?"

"It's his heart."

"His heart," she repeats.

Nodding, I shift back to the subject at hand, or the subject about what's not on her hand. "I need you to wear the rings, Trina. If Lloyd stops by and you're not wearing them, that's a discussion neither of us wants or needs."

Her eyes widen. "He's coming here today?"

Feeling as though I finally have her full attention, I shrug. "He's unpredictable."

"I locked the rings in my desk drawer." She drops her gaze to her left hand. "I'll put them back on, sir, but we need to agree on what to tell everyone."

"Everyone?" I question. "Like who?"

"Like Kay," she tosses out the name of one of our designers.

Kay is a holdover from Lloyd's days. She's still working on designs that hit the market hard decades ago. I haven't used one of her ideas since I took control of the company.

"We'll tell Kay, and anyone else who asks, that we're married."

It sounds reasonable, but judging by the look of confusion on my wife's face, I missed the mark with my suggestion.

"We'll tell her that it started with innocent flirting, and then we went out for a drink after work," she says softly. "That led to dinner and a night of talking. Fate took over from there, and it became a whirlwind romance."

Impressed, I nod. "I can work with that."

"Three months from now, I'll tell the staff that…"

"You realized that my attitude is more than you can deal with," I interrupt. "You decided to leave me because the flame that was burning brightly was extinguished by my raging level of assholeness."

"Assholeness?" she repeats. "That actually fits."

That should sting, but it's fuel for my erection. I harden even more.

"Put your wedding rings back on," I say to chase her out of my office.

I don't need my wife to glance down to catch my body's reaction to her.

"Yes, sir," she says with a smirk.

Jesus. How the fuck will I survive being fake married to this woman when all I can think about is that kiss we shared last night and how I want more?

CHAPTER FIFTEEN

Trina

I CIRCLE the block for the third time, gazing up as I pass Graham's building.

He left the office before me.

I'd say he snuck out, but Mr. Locke isn't a sneak. He's bold and unapologetic. He's also forgetful at times. That happened this afternoon when he left his office while I was on my coffee break.

I came back, plopped my ass down in the comfy leather chair behind my desk, and started talking to him about a shipment of watches bound for San Francisco.

When he didn't huff out an acknowledgment, I finally turned to find his office empty.

It wasn't until twenty minutes later that he sent me a text message telling me that he had gone home to work.

I have to go up to the penthouse to pretend to be his wife, but I need another minute as my alter ego Trina Shaw before I do that.

"Mrs. Locke?"

Hearing that stops me so abruptly that the person behind me bumps into the back of me.

She doesn't apologize. All I get from her is a sneer as she rounds me and continues her trek down the crowded sidewalk.

"Mrs. Locke, over here."

I search the faces that pass me, wondering who the hell knows that I'm married to Graham.

When I see the doorman with his arm raised in the air, I sigh.

I wave back at him. "Hey."

I've never had a doorman, so I have zero understanding of how to greet one properly. I assume that I'm supposed to put some money in his hand when he does open the door for me.

I lucked out yesterday when I arrived with my suitcase. I snuck in after another tenant. This morning, there wasn't a doorman in sight when I left to go to work.

"Are you lost?" he asks with a tilt of his head.

The answer to that is too complicated to get into with him, so I shake my head.

"You've passed the building three times in the past fifteen minutes," he points out.

Considering the fact that I'm wearing heels, that's impressive.

I've never joined a gym. My workouts have always consisted of strolling around the city and doing lunges in my living room. When I feel inclined to lift weights, I go to Brooklyn since my sister, Clara, keeps five-pound hand weights in the kitchen of the bakery.

I fit in a sisterly visit and an arm workout all at once.

"I do my best thinking on my walk to work," he admits. "I sense you've got a lot on your mind."

He has no idea.

A million thoughts are racing through my head, including the way Graham kissed me last night.

I was going to bring it up at work, but it felt out of place.

Now, I'm not sure I should mention it at all. He was playing the part of the devoted husband. I'm not an expert on kissing, but to me, it was an Oscar-worthy performance.

I drop my gaze to the doorman's nametag. "I was getting my steps in for the day, Eugene."

He looks at my wrist. "Do you have one of those fancy watches that count steps, heart rate, and calories?"

If I did, I'd never look at it.

Simple is best in my world.

I take as many steps as I need to get where I'm going. My heart rate has only spiked recently when I've been near my husband. As for calories, I eat as healthy as I can, except for when I go to Brooklyn.

I can't walk out of the bakery without sampling something. That's tradition.

"I don't." I turn my arm to show him the Abdons watch on my wrist.

I found it at a vintage store called Past Over years ago. I didn't realize what a true treasure it was until I started working for Mr. Locke.

He pushes up the sleeve of his jacket to show me a watch with a black leather band. "Me either."

I note the time on his watch and realize that if I'm going to cook dinner again, I need to get upstairs.

"I'll walk you to the elevator," Eugene offers.

I loop my hand around his offered elbow. "Thank you, kind sir."

"It's my pleasure, Mrs. Locke."

I know this will cost me a dollar or two, but I stroll

through the lobby next to him, feeling slightly less lost than I did ten minutes ago.

I STEP off of the elevator to find my husband and Lloyd standing side-by-side.

Graham has lost the tie and jacket he had on at the office. The button-down shirt he's wearing is open at the collar. His shirtsleeves are still held in place by cufflinks, so I'm not going to get the bonus treat of a view of his bare arms today.

I take a second to wonder whether the tattoo on his forearm is the only one he has.

I'll never find out.

"Trina!" Mr. Abdon comes at me with his arms outstretched. "I was getting worried."

My gaze drifts to Graham as I let Lloyd take me in a hug.

My boss doesn't look like a man who is concerned about his tardy spouse. He's sporting his signature *'what the fuck?'* look.

I didn't realize I had a curfew.

I pull back from Lloyd. "I'll get started on dinner."

I arranged for a grocery delivery less than an hour ago. I decided we'd eat salmon tonight with rice pilaf and steamed broccoli.

"No need." Lloyd beams as he looks at me. "I'm having dinner brought in."

My gaze volleys from him to Graham. "That's not necessary. I can change and have dinner on the table in thirty minutes."

Lloyd holds a fist to the center of his chest. "I'll be long gone in thirty minutes."

Given the condition of his health, I try not to take that literally. "What do you mean?"

"I have plans," he explains. "I'll be out for a couple of hours. That will give you two enough time to enjoy your special meal and perhaps some dessert."

He tosses my husband a wink.

I narrow my gaze, concerned that he's overdoing it. "You're going out?"

"I'm leaving now." He moves to press the elevator call button. "Don't wait up for me. I promise I'll head straight to my room once I'm home."

CHAPTER SIXTEEN

GRAHAM

I'D BOW out of this dinner, but I suspect Lloyd is paying the woman who showed up thirty minutes ago to spy on Trina and me.

She's wearing a chef's coat and is preparing something in the kitchen, but the way she keeps popping back into the dining room is a dead giveaway that her job entails more than putting food on the table tonight.

Since she arrived, she's asked me three times if I need anything.

The only thing I *need* is for my wife to reappear.

She ran off in the direction of my bedroom after Lloyd left.

I expected as much. I've asked a great deal of Miss Shaw the past few days, but she is being generously compensated, so I expect her to at least make an appearance before the night is over.

"I brought a bottle of wine," the chef announces as she

peers around the corner yet again. "Should I open that now, or would you rather I wait for your wife to join us?"

I'd rather it was a bottle of aged scotch, but liars can't be choosers.

"I'm sorry that took so long," Trina apologizes as she approaches from behind the chef. "I wanted to change before dinner."

I didn't bother to swap out my suit pants and button-down shirt. I can't say the same for my wife.

Her skirt and blouse have been replaced with a red dress that's cinched at her waist with a thin belt. The shoes on her feet are strappy with low heels.

She's braided her hair to one side.

I not only feel underdressed, but I feel unworthy of this.

She's fucking breathtaking.

"Do I look all right?" she asks before she spins in a circle.

"You're beautiful," the chef whispers. "Wow."

I wholeheartedly agree with her assessment, so I chime in. "You look lovely, Trina."

She smiles before her attention falls on the face of the chef. "I'm Trina. It's really nice to meet you."

That sets the gray-haired woman back a step. She skims a palm over the front of her white chef's jacket before she offers her hand to my wife. "I'm Bette."

They exchange a soft handshake as Trina closes her eyes briefly. "Whatever you're cooking smells like heaven. Can I help you with anything?"

Bette lets out a light-hearted chuckle. "That's not necessary, but thank you."

"If you change your mind, you know where to find me." Trina smiles.

The chef glances in my direction. "Should I open the wine now, Mr. Locke?"

"Please." I nod. "You can serve dinner as soon as it's ready."

"You can't rush perfection," Trina chimes in. "Don't feel the need to hurry, Bette. Graham and I want you to take all the time you need."

I don't want that.

I want to strip that dress from my wife's body and take her to bed, but since that's not an option, I want to eat dinner and race out of here with an excuse about needing to take care of a work issue.

Surely, Lloyd won't question that when he receives his surveillance report from Bette.

As soon as the chef is out of view, Trina turns to me. "I didn't want her to feel pressured. I know what it's like when you want something done right now, sir."

The fact that '*sir*' keeps popping out from between her bee-stung lips is a problem, but I'm not going to correct her this time.

It's rousing something within me.

Something dangerous and completely out of the realm of possibility.

I can't fuck my wife.

I chant that to myself while she studies my face waiting for me to respond.

I'm saved by the reappearance of Bette with a bottle of Merlot in one hand and two wine glasses in the other.

She's not only bothersome, but she's also laser fast.

I wait while she pours a splash of wine in one of the glasses and offers it to me for my approval. I skip past the expected sniff and small taste and instead gulp down every last drop.

"I take that as a sign it's good to go," Bette mutters under her breath.

She half-fills the other glass for my wife before she does the same with mine.

As Bette heads back to the kitchen, Trina turns to me and raises her glass in the air. "To red wine."

"To red wine and red dresses." I follow that with a slow sip as I rake my gaze over my wife.

Leave it to me to marry the most stunning woman on the planet. She just also happens to be the woman who wants nothing to do with me outside of the office and our temporary arrangement.

―――

FIVE FUCKING COURSES.

I had to sit through five fucking courses staring at Trina while she savored the meal.

The food was fine, but the experience of watching my assistant eat was sensual. She closed her eyes after several bites, moaned her approval, and kept running her fingertip over her bottom lip.

I suspect that was designed to catch any wayward crumbs, but my dick didn't get that memo.

It took it upon itself to get hard and stay hard as I watched my wife eat her way through five dishes that I can barely remember at this point.

Bette cleared the table ten minutes ago, and now, she's peering at us from around the corner.

She may be a great cook, but her skills in being stealthy are sorely lacking.

Trina leans her forearms on the table to close the distance between us.

The movement results in an unexpected gift for me. My wife's breasts are pushed together, giving me a clear view of the top of them.

I reach for my wine glass, finish what's left, and then for good measure, I finish Trina's wine too.

She shoots me a frown, I think.

I only catch the briefest glimpse of it as I tear my gaze away from her tits.

"Graham," she whispers my name, and *Jesus Christ*, I'm ready to crawl over the table, bend her over and take her right here and now.

I've always found solace in the soft sound of her everyday speaking voice, but this is next level.

"Yes?" I try to mimic her tone, but my voice comes out sounding strangled.

Her blonde brows perk. "Are you all right?"

That depends. Are we speaking in general terms, or is the question rooted in my body's desperate need for her?

She doesn't wait for me to answer. "Do you think Bette is spying on us?"

Leave it to my trusting wife to deduce that two hours into this dinner. I sense she always gives people the benefit of the doubt. Her first impression of Bette was that of an experienced private chef. Mine was more cynical. I knew that Lloyd had an ulterior motive for this dinner.

Bette has likely been texting him updates throughout the evening. I've caught her with her gaze locked on her phone's screen a few times.

"I'd bet everything I own on it," I say with confidence.

"Even the pelican statue?"

"What the fuck?" I whisper shout. "What are you talking about?"

I'm wealthy to a point well past obscenity, but I have never sunk a dime into a pelican statue. That much I know.

I glance in Bette's direction to catch her fingers flying over her phone's screen.

Fuck.

She's likely mistaking this for an argument.

I cover by grabbing hold of my wife's hands, her very soft, perfect hands.

That draws her gaze to my face.

"I don't own a pelican statue," I point out, although to be fair, if Trina asked me to commission one from the greatest sculptor alive, I'd give it serious consideration.

I blame that thought on the wine.

It's never my drink of choice. When I indulge in too much wine, my mind wanders and gets trapped in places too emotional for my liking.

"You do," she counters.

Pasting a smile on my face for Bette's benefit, I grit out three words, "I don't, dear."

Trina's lips curve up into a grin. "Oh, but you do, darling."

I squeeze her hands, not hard, but enough to keep her attention trained on my face. "You're mistaken."

"No, you are." A sugary sweet smile accompanies those words.

I want to kiss that off her face.

"I'll bet you that you have one," she says, tilting her head.

"What do I get when I win that bet?" I ask, even though I know I'm already victorious.

She studies me, likely contemplating what the hell she can wager that I would want.

Her.

The answer is that simple.

I want to kiss her again, so I take the initiative. I lower my voice. "I don't own a pelican statue, Trina. I know I'm right.

If I win this bet, you'll have a drink with me at the bar across the street."

"You have alcohol here."

I lean even closer to her. "Bette is here."

She drops her chin in a subtle nod. "Understood."

"And if you win?" I question. "If I own a pelican statue…" I chuckle my way through that statement. "What do I have to do?"

"Dishes for a month."

CHAPTER SEVENTEEN

Graham

"FOR THE RECORD, I have a dishwasher, and I would have hired someone to put the dishes in it."

Trina peers at me over the top of the glass that's perched at her lips. "It's called loading it, Graham, and I'm pretty sure you could have handled it on your own."

"I'll never know." I tip my glass of smooth scotch at her before I savor a sip.

I won our bet with ease.

When pressed, I asked my wife to show me the so-called pelican statue. She got up, marched toward the hallway that leads to the east wing, and then turned and sat back down.

That's when she told me that she'd like a martini, dry with two olives.

It's currently still in her hand as she watches me.

I wait until she takes her first sip before I respond to her comment. "I know how to load a dishwasher."

She sets the glass on the wooden table that separates us.

It's small and in the corner of the bar that we came to ten minutes ago.

"Prove it," she challenges.

"No need."

"No need?" she parrots my words. "Or no knowledge? I bet you're one of those people who load it improperly. You probably put the bowls in wrong, so when the cycle is done, they've flipped and are filled with murky water."

I disregard everything she just said, save for one thing. "Another bet? What's the wager this time around?"

Her gaze shifts from my face to something behind me.

In any normal circumstance, I'd ignore that, but curiosity turns my head to the side. I catch a glimpse of a guy in a suit. He's around my age, but his taste in clothing isn't as refined as mine. Neither is his demeanor. The not-so-subtle wave of his hand is directed at my wife.

"A friend of yours?" I ask as I turn back to face Trina.

I catch her hand falling to her lap.

Apparently, the greeting was mutual.

"No," she answers curtly. "He's not my friend."

I should find that amusing, but I don't. She's here with me. Fake married or not, I'm her date for the evening.

I turn my entire body to face the guy and give him a hearty wave. It's not a fist or open-handed. Instead, it's a front handed motion meant to send a clear message that I'm wearing a wedding ring.

In an attempt to drive home that point, I call out to him. "Your first drink is on me... and my wife."

"Graham!"

The shock in Trina's voice turns me back toward her. "Yes, dear?"

That's enough to get a smile out of her. "Why did you do that?"

"Do what?"

My attempt to play dumb doesn't sit well with my wife. She narrows her eyes. "I don't see the problem with acknowledging a stranger's attempt to be friendly. It would have been rude to ignore him."

"Not rude," I disagree with a shake of my head. "Expected. This is Manhattan, Trina. Do you know how many times a day a guy like that gets shot down when he tries to make a move on a woman?"

Her arms cross her chest. "He wasn't making a move, Graham."

"He was."

She takes a sip from her drink. "Since you're the self-proclaimed expert on this, tell me how many times a day do you get shot down when you make a move on a woman."

I chuckle. "Never."

"Never?" She laughs. "Be honest, Graham. How many times?"

I push my drink aside so I can reach over and snatch my wife's hand in mine. My touch is much less gentle than it was at the penthouse. I want her attention. I want all of it.

Staring directly into her eyes, I clear my throat. "I've never had the unfortunate experience of being turned down by a woman, Trina."

Her gaze travels over my face before her eyes lock on mine. "I'd turn you down."

"Liar," I accuse.

That sets her head back in a roar of laughter. "I'm not lying. You're not my type."

That stings more than it should.

Naturally, my ego won't let it slide, so I press, "I'm not your type?"

"No," she answers swiftly.

"What's your type?" I question, skeptical of whether or not she's being truthful.

"He is." She tilts her chin toward the bar.

She has to be referring to the guy in the cheap suit. I want to get out of my chair and haul him out of here so she can't steal another glance at him, but I stay seated because I have no claim to her. She may be my wife, but that's temporary and in name only.

"He's successful," she points out. "But not too successful."

"That's a thing?" I hold in a laugh.

She looks beyond my shoulder again. "His suit didn't cost a small fortune, and his phone isn't in his hand. To me, that means that he values other things more than his image, and in his world, work can wait."

In other words, the guy at the bar is the polar opposite of me.

Her gaze gets stuck on him again, but the smile on her face tells me something is happening. I see the way her hand reaches up to skim over her hair.

Goddammit.

My wife's not-so-secret admirer must be on the move.

"Thanks for the drink," a voice says from behind me. "It's not often that anyone in this city does something like that. I appreciate it."

I don't wait for Trina to respond. Instead, I turn and look up at the guy who has his eyes pinned to my wife. "No problem. Enjoy your night."

"You look familiar." He points a finger at Trina. "Have we met?"

You have to be fucking kidding me.

I'm sitting right here. She has a diamond on her finger the size of Saturn.

Trina smiles. "I don't think so."

He studies her carefully. "I swear I know you. I'm going to go sit back down and figure out when we first met."

I turn to look up at him. "You do that."

He ignores me because my wife is so fucking beautiful he can't tear his eyes away from her. "I'll be back when I figure it out."

Trina's gaze trails him as he walks away.

I finish what's left of my drink in one gulp. "We're done. It's time to go home."

CHAPTER EIGHTEEN

TRINA

IF PRESSED, I'd give myself an eight out of ten when it comes to reading people. I credit that to the fact that I grew up in a small house with fourteen other family members. Not everyone was direct, so I developed a sixth sense when reading between the lines of what someone says and finding the hidden clues in their demeanor.

If I'm not mistaken, my husband was jealous when the guy at the bar came over to talk to us.

It was another instance of someone recognizing me from my family's bakery. I know that for a fact because I worked the counter one Saturday afternoon a few months ago to help out, and he ordered a birthday cake for his sister.

We flirted, he left without asking for my number, and I waited for him to call the bakery to ask someone there how to reach me.

That never happened.

I could have confessed all of that at the bar, but I decided to keep it to myself since I was having a drink with my husband.

I glance over at Graham as we ride the elevator up to his penthouse.

He hasn't said one word to me since we left the bar.

This is as pissy a p.m. as I've ever seen, but I don't point that out because I'm still clinging to the very slim hope that after this charade is over, I'll still have a job at Abdons.

It may not be as an assistant to the CEO, but there are plenty of executives who could use someone with my expertise.

The elevator slows as it nears our destination.

Graham finally turns to look at me. "I'm sure Lloyd is asleep. I'm going to call it a night."

Relief flows through me.

I'm looking forward to a hot shower and an episode or two of the show I've been trying to binge-watch since back when I was single a few days ago.

"Me too," I respond with a smile. "By the way, thanks for the martini."

It was one of the best martinis I've had.

I prefer to sip a cocktail, but since my husband turned into a major grouch after that guy at the bar spoke to us, I had to down the delicious concoction in one gulp before we raced out of the place.

I suspect I'll be fast asleep within the hour.

"Not a problem," he says in that non-romantic way he has.

My smile droops because why waste it on a man who is looking at me with a scowl?

The ding of the elevator draws both of our gazes forward.

As the doors slide open, I feel Graham's hand wrap

around mine. I glance down in disbelief. I thought I was done playing Mrs. Locke for the night.

"The lovebirds are home!"

I look up again to find Mr. Abdon standing in the foyer, dressed in a red robe over black silk pajamas. He's holding a glass of something in his hand. My guess is that it's scotch.

Graham draws my hand up to his mouth to lightly graze his lips over my knuckles.

That shouldn't make me weak in the knees, but it does. I could blame it on the martini, but why lie to myself?

I like when my husband's lips brush against my skin. It makes me wonder what it would feel like in places he can't see.

I shake off that thought and delve back into the role of a lifetime.

"Lloyd," I say his name as Graham leads me off the elevator. "It's late. Why are you still up?"

I trust that doesn't sound accusatory. I didn't expect to see him. I was counting on making a dash for Mr. Locke's bedroom as soon as the elevator's doors opened.

"How could I not stay up to say goodnight to two of my favorite people?" He asks. "Was dinner to your liking? Bette said you left. Am I right to assume you went dancing?"

Hope swims in his eyes, so I drop my gaze to the floor as I tug my hand free from Graham's. The lies are weighing heavier on me as each moment passes. I hope Graham takes my silence as a hint so he can answer Lloyd.

"Dinner was delicious," Graham says. "We snuck out to get a drink at a special spot."

Special?

The only thing special about it is that it's a hop, skip, and jump from the lobby doors of this building.

"Sela and I would go to a bar in Greenwich Village every

Friday night after work," he begins before he takes a breath. "It was called Lawtons back then. Now, it's Tin Anchor. So much has changed."

Sorrow edges his words, so I glance at him.

"Time has a way of changing things," Graham offers.

"That's the truth," Lloyd punctuates his words with a nod of his chin. "Some changes are for the better, right, Bull?"

Bull?

My head snaps in Graham's direction because what the hell? Bull? Is that a nickname?

In some abstract way, it fits.

Mr. Locke is bull-headed. He doesn't take bullshit from anyone. I bet he's like a bull in bed.

Wait. What?

I shake off any thought of what my boss is like between the sheets.

"Some changes are for the better," Graham agrees without a glance in my direction. "Why don't I see you to your room, Lloyd?"

"I am getting tired." Lloyd turns to me. "I promise I won't keep him for too long, Trina. He'll be beside you in bed before you know it."

I ignore that last remark because I'll be alone in bed before I know it and for the foreseeable future.

"Sweet dreams, Lloyd." I move to kiss his cheek. "I'll see you in the morning."

"You can count on that." He squeezes my shoulder. "Goodnight, Trina."

Graham reaches for Lloyd's forearm as he leads the older man down the hallway toward the guestroom without a single glance back.

CHAPTER NINETEEN

Trina

I POCKET my wedding rings just as I swing open the door to the café that Aurora works at.

I had brunch with Lloyd and Graham before my husband announced that he would be meeting with a watch designer who is only in Manhattan for a day. Lloyd scoffed at the idea of hiring yet another new designer, so he insisted on tagging along to the meeting with Graham.

Given that it's Saturday, I was surprised but grateful to have a few hours away from my make-believe life.

Stopping in here to see Aurora helps me two-fold. I get to see her beautiful face, and I can pick up a cup of Clara's favorite coffee to take to Brooklyn with me.

My sister never complains that the coffee is lukewarm by the time I hand it to her. She always pops off the lid, shoves it into the microwave, and sixty seconds later, she's enjoying her first sip.

Bringing her a coffee a few times a month is the least I can do.

Clara gave up her job as an accountant and stepped in to run the bakery after my folks retired. They both still show up to work in the kitchen or behind the counter for a few hours each week, but it's Clara who handles everything from hiring staff to ordering supplies.

She said she's always known she had sugar running through her veins because managing the bakery makes her happier than anything else.

I look to where Aurora is busily making a drink that is topped with what looks like whipped cream and cinnamon.

I may have to break out of my routine and go for one of those today.

As soon as she spots me, her face lights up. "Trina! Hey!"

I raise a hand to wave at her from the back of the line. "How are you?"

"Busy," she replies with a chuckle. "I've missed you. I stopped by your apartment last night, but you weren't home. Did you have a hot date?"

Both women in front of me, who are waiting to place their orders, turn to look.

I smile at them and shrug. "No hot date. No date at all."

It comes out sounding way more awkward than I intend.

Aurora hands the beverage she prepared to a man in a suit before she replies, "I guess that was wishful thinking on my part. Given how many brothers and sisters you have, you must have been hanging out with one of them."

I tell myself that I'm not lying to her if I don't say another word on the subject.

I wait patiently while she prepares the orders of the two women in line in front of me.

One approaches me after she picks up her latte. "If you're

single, I have a brother you should meet. I can give you his number."

I laugh that off. "I'm sure he's great, but I'm not looking for anything right now."

"She's taking some me time." Aurora curls her fingers to toss air quotes around the last two words. "That means no he time."

"I like that," the woman says, grinning. "I should try that sometime."

"And I should try something new," I begin before I wink at Aurora as I approach the counter. "I'll have something decadent with whip cream and cinnamon on top. Make it two. I want to surprise my sister."

"You've got it." Aurora snatches up a paper cup to write my name on the side. "Do you have time for a quick visit before you head to Brooklyn? My break is in five minutes."

"I have all day," I say happily.

I plan on savoring the next few hours before I go back to the penthouse.

"Perfect." Aurora beams. "I'll make your drink, and then after we chat, I'll whip up something extra special for Clara."

WITH A BELLY FULL of blueberry cobbler and a heart filled with happiness after spending two hours at the bakery with one of my sisters, I slide my wedding rings back on.

Adjusting the diamond so it's centered on my finger, I sigh.

I'd never admit it to my husband, but I'm getting used to wearing the rings. When I get married for real one day, I already know that I'll never take my rings off.

I sense that they add an extra level of bonding between

couples who have devoted themselves to each other for the right reasons.

Unlike Graham and I.

Our marriage is meant to pull the wool over someone's eyes, someone I admire and respect.

"Mrs. Locke," Eugene calls to me as I approach the lobby doors. "How are you, this fine Saturday?"

I perk an eyebrow. "You work on weekends?"

"Every second Saturday," he explains as he reaches for the curved steel handle of one of the lobby doors. "The trade-off is that I get to spend Monday with my wife."

I breeze past him. "That sounds like it works out well."

"You know it," he says.

Shoving a hand in the front pocket of my jeans, I tug out a five dollar bill and offer it to him. "Thank you, Eugene."

He waves it away with a swat of his hand in the air. "Your husband told me earlier today that I'm not to accept any more tips from his beautiful wife."

I reach for his hand and tuck the money into his palm. "It's our little secret then."

His face beams with a bright smile. "I'll keep it to myself."

"Is he home?" I question as Eugene walks next to me through the lobby. "He was going into the office for at least part of the day."

"He left with Mr. Abdon a couple of hours ago." He drops the volume of his voice. "I've been at my post since, and they haven't snuck past me."

Breathing a sigh of relief, I nod my head. "That gives me time to freshen up before they get back."

"Not that you need it." He winks. "If I haven't mentioned it, you're a breath of fresh air, Mrs. Locke. It's good to see Mr. Locke happy."

My head snaps in Eugene's direction as he pushes the elevator call button. "He's happy?"

He leans a touch closer to me. "Just between us, your husband didn't always stop to say hello when he arrived home."

"He does now?"

"Each and every time." He nods. "It seems that you brought some much needed sunshine into his life."

Even though I'm well aware that my husband would never acknowledge that, I like knowing it.

CHAPTER TWENTY

Graham

I'D SAY this is a sight for sore eyes, but it's more apt to call it a sight for my aching dick.

My wife is sporting jean cut-offs and a light blue T-shirt as she naps on one of the uncomfortable couches in my living room.

This is not the outfit she had on when she took off out of her earlier. I should know. I thought she looked amazing in the jeans and sweater she was wearing then.

This getup she's in now is next level.

I've never considered myself a leg man, but *goddammit*, Trina's legs are fucking perfection. They are long, tanned, and bent slightly at the knees as she rests on her side with her hands tucked beneath her face.

"Look at that angel," Lloyd whispers as he points at the vision in front of us. "I think you married up, Bull."

I didn't just marry up. I married a woman who is better than me in every possible way.

She stirs slightly.

"Carry her to bed," he demands. "Scoop up your bride and take her to bed."

My head snaps in his direction. "What?"

"Do it," he urges with an elbow in my rib cage. "You two could use a few moments alone before dinner."

I catch the wink he sends my way.

If I'm not mistaken, he's telling me in a not so discreet way to take my wife to the bedroom for a late afternoon fuck.

I'm game, but since Trina and I are married for all the wrong reasons, that's not going to happen.

She told me to my face that I'm not her type.

I still highly doubt that, but now is not the time to dwell on whether or not Miss Shaw finds me as fuckable as I find her.

"Let's leave her be," I suggest so I can get the hell out of this room.

I want to jump into a cold shower and conjure up a mental image of anything other than my wife.

"Why?" Lloyd perks both of his graying brows. "Your bed has to be more comfortable than that couch."

The floor is more comfortable than that couch, as is the concrete sidewalk in front of the building.

I can tell that he's not going to drop this, so I give in.

I move toward my assistant to slide a hand under her to grab her waist. She wiggles, but her eyes stay closed.

I scoop my other hand under her knees and instantly have her up in my arms.

That's enough to jar her awake.

Her eyelids pop open, and the sight she's greeted with is my face. "Graham?"

For fuck's sake.

If I thought her voice was sexy before, this just woken version of it is enough to make me come in my pants.

That hasn't happened since I was a teenager.

I draw in a deep breath to try and conquer my need for her. "The bed is a much better place to have a nap."

Her lazy gaze drifts from my face to where Lloyd is standing behind me.

"Graham's going to take you to bed," he announces with a chuckle. "I'm headed to my room. I'll see you, newlyweds, in a couple of hours."

Trina's fingers drift over my shoulder to the back of my neck. They whisper over my hairline.

Her touch is soft. It feels intimate in a way I'm not expecting.

I glance at her face again to find her staring at me.

"We'll see you later, Lloyd," I say without tearing my gaze away from my wife.

I carry her silently to my bedroom, wishing that I could slam the door behind us, strip her, and spend the next two hours consummating this marriage.

AS SOON AS SHE CAN, Trina slips from my arms and lands on my bedroom floor on her bare feet.

I rake her over only to stop midway because it's obvious that she enjoyed the ride in here. Her nipples have furled into tight little points beneath her T-shirt.

I'd trade half of my fortune for the chance to get my teeth around one.

Who the fuck am I kidding? I'd hand over everything I own and all of my future income to taste not only her tits but the rest of her too.

Her arms jump to cross her chest. "Why are you looking at me like that?"

Honesty may be the best policy, but if I confess that I want to fuck her raw, I sense she'll pack up her suitcase and run for the hills.

I divert because keeping this *marriage* on track is my priority. "You're going to be happy to know that Kay's latest design is part of the spring collection."

Her face lights up. "Are you fucking kidding me right now?"

I work to hold in a chuckle. "I'm not fucking kidding you right now."

She bounces on her feet. That sends her already messy hair tumbling around her shoulders.

I glance down because of my ongoing effort to tame my dick when I'm in the same room as her.

"Does she know?"

I look up to find her hands on her hips and those nipples still at rapt attention. "No."

"Can I be there when you tell her?" she asks like I'm about to hand Kay the keys to the Abdons kingdom.

I hold those tightly in my palm and have no intention of ever letting them out of my grasp.

"You can tell her."

"What?" Her eyes lock on mine. "I can tell her? Are you serious, Graham?"

If something like this brings my wife joy, I'll make the dreams of every one of our employees come true, just so she can spread the good news.

"We'll go over the details on Monday morning." I eye up the door that leads to the bedroom I've been staying in.

I'm in desperate need of that cold shower now.

"I'll look forward to that, sir."

Sir. Again.

Fuck my fucking hard cock.

"I'll see you at dinner, Trina." I inch back a few steps toward the bedroom door. "We're having dinner at Nova tonight with Lloyd."

"That's super fancy." She smiles. "I'll pick out something extra nice to wear."

She could wrap a potato sack around her body, and she'd be a vision of beauty.

"All right," I half-cough out as I step back yet again.

"See you later, husband."

My lips curl into a half-ass smile. "Later, wife."

I finally open the door and retreat into the hallway. Sucking in a deep breath, I graze a hand over the outline of my erection through my pants.

A cold shower won't fix this. I need to circle my cock with my fist and pump one out.

I don't give a shit if it's appropriate or not, my wife is going to be the inspiration for every fantasy I have until the day she divorces me.

CHAPTER TWENTY-ONE

TRINA

I ATE all of my dinner with my left hand in my lap.

That's because I know far too many people in New York City, and I didn't want any of them spotting the sparkler on my left hand. I'm still in the process of crafting a speech to recite to my family as soon as I'm divorced.

It won't be easy, but I'm hoping that once they hear that I did it mostly to make Mr. Abdon happy, they'll understand.

The money is a great perk, though.

"Where to now?" Lloyd spins in a circle on the sidewalk outside of the restaurant.

He toasted to our marriage so many times during dinner that I lost track.

Graham and I both lifted our wine glasses silently each time, clinking them together before taking a sip of the bold red wine.

I had to pretend to sip after the sixth toast so I could manage to leave the restaurant on my own two feet.

"Home," Graham mutters.

"It's late," I chime in to second my husband's suggestion. "I can make us some herbal tea before you go to bed."

Both men turn to look at me.

Lloyd's gaze is soft.

Graham can't seem to take his eyes off the front of my dress. I admit the neckline plunges, but it's the nicest little black dress I own, and I wanted to look extra special since Mr. Abdon dropped a few hundred dollars on the meal we just ate. Most of that was spent on wine.

"Look at you two." Lloyd's hand traces circles in the air as if he's a magician about to unveil a hidden rabbit. "You're eager to hit the hay."

I can't speak for my boss, but I'm ready to call it a night.

Today has felt like four days compressed into one.

I need a break and something stronger than herbal tea. I wish I were at home so I could knock on Aurora's door for a hot cup of coffee and one of her smiles.

"I'll get a car to pick us up." Graham's fingers fly over his phone's screen. "The wait shouldn't be long."

A shiver runs through me as I nod. I didn't think to grab a sweater to ward off the cool evening breeze. I had to rush to get ready when Graham sent me a text message telling me to meet him and Lloyd in the living room.

The warm shower I took was way too long, and that's not because I spent thirty minutes conditioning my hair.

I touched myself as the water ran over me.

Thoughts of my husband may have been playing in my mind. It was hard not to think about the way his hands felt on my body as he carried me to his bedroom or the way he stared at me after he set me down on my feet.

"You're cold." Graham steps toward me. "You're cold, aren't you, Trina?"

Before I can get a word out, his suit jacket is off of his body and wrapped around mine. He adjusts the lapels, taking a moment to slide his fingers down until they almost brush against my breasts.

I stare at him. "Thank you, Graham."

"Back in my day we'd call that chivalrous," Lloyd says from where he's standing to the left of us. "You've come a long way from the boy you used to be, Bull."

I look into my husband's eyes. "Bull? That's your nickname?"

"Was," he gently corrects me as he once again adjusts the jacket wrapped around me.

"We agreed that I'd stop calling him that around the office. I got used to that, but now that I'm retired, it slips out," Mr. Abdon explains with a chuckle.

I want to get to the bottom of this, so I press on, "Lloyd, why Bull? Where did that come from?"

Graham's index finger darts to my chin. He turns my head a touch until I'm looking at him again. "It's a very long and boring story that's not worth getting into."

I glance over his shoulder at the few cars that are approaching us. "I think we have time. It doesn't look like our ride is within sight."

Lloyd clears his throat to gain my attention again. "It started when he was a lot younger."

Whatever he says next is lost under the sound of my husband's voice. "I played football in high school. I picked up the nickname then."

"Graham," Lloyd snaps out.

My gaze volleys between both men. It's obvious that Graham isn't telling me the whole story behind the name, but Lloyd wants to, so I focus on him. "How did you hear about the name if it was Graham's nickname in high school?"

Lloyd glances at Graham. I've seen that look only a handful of times in the past, and it's always been in the office when Lloyd has been primed to drop some juicy details about a business deal.

This isn't a business deal, though. This is Graham's past.

"Lloyd was in the stands for a few games," he says in a rush as his gaze darts over his shoulder. "Where's the damn car?"

"To watch you play?"

Graham looks at me again. "It was his alma mater. He used to play on the same team back in his day."

I search Mr. Abdon's face for some truth, but he drops his chin down. "That's right."

Graham breathes a heavy and very audible sigh of relief. "That's our car. It's time to go home."

And just like that, the discussion about my husband's past has come to an abrupt end, and I have way more questions than answers about the man I married.

CHAPTER TWENTY-TWO

Graham

"I'M SORRY, GRAHAM."

I squeeze my eyes shut when I hear the emotion in Lloyd's voice. I didn't fucking want this to happen. My intention wasn't to silence him in front of the restaurant, but I'm a huge proponent of letting sleeping dogs lie.

I don't need or want Miss Shaw to gain insight into the person I used to be.

I left that guy behind when I graduated from college and started working an entry-level position at Abdons.

I've wished for a hell of a long time that Lloyd would drop the nickname I carried with me for years, but he's still clinging to it. I know why. It's part habit and part nostalgia.

Lloyd wishes his past was his present, but time can't maintain that.

Life changes.

People change. I'm proof of that.

I turn and face him. "No need to apologize."

He nods sagely. "You're not comfortable telling Trina about…"

"No," I cut him off before he gets the two words I hate the most out of his mouth.

The past.

"She'd understand," he states as though life is that simple.

Maybe she would, or perhaps she'd judge me, but it doesn't matter. I'm tied to Trina for three months, and then we'll part ways. She'll leave with more than a million dollars, and I'll walk away knowing I gave Lloyd something he wanted.

That's the chance to see me settled down with a woman he believes I'm worthy of.

I'm not, but I'm keeping that to myself in the same way I've kept my past to myself.

"At least consider telling her," he says as he adjusts the collar of the pajama top he's wearing.

I waited in a chair in the corner of the guestroom while he was in the bathroom getting ready for bed. I couldn't leave things unsaid because what if this night is his last?

I've asked repeatedly if he'd like to see a heart specialist now that he's back in New York. That's been strictly selfish on my part because I don't want the old man to leave me.

He insists that he doesn't need a second, third or fourth opinion. He knows his fate.

I move to face him. "Lloyd, I appreciate that you believe in transparency in marriage, but this is different."

"It's not." He places a shaking hand on my shoulder. "You're assuming that Trina doesn't have the capacity to understand who you once were. If a woman truly loves a man, she'll see past his weaknesses to his growth and maturity. You're not the same bull-headed kid I met years ago."

I fight off a smile. "I sure as hell hope not."

"Don't get me wrong." He brushes his hand over the front of my shirt. "You're still just as stubborn now, but you only dig in your heels when you believe strongly in something."

I see a path that will lead me out of this conversation, so I jump on it. "You're talking about Kay?"

He huffs out a stuttered laugh. "I'm not, but I made the right decision about her design. It's what the market wants right now, Bull."

"You know how I feel about that." I chuckle. "My opinion hasn't changed, Lloyd. Her timepiece is dated. We'd do better with one of the designs I recommend."

"I still have the final say," he reminds me. "We are going with Kay's design. You have the job of telling her that."

"Trina's going to handle it." I cross my arms over my chest. "Her face lit up like the Eiffel Tower when I told her she could break the good news to Kay."

He studies me as a slow smile creeps over his lips. "You're already learning the pleasure of sacrificing for your wife."

"Kay's a friend to Trina," I say to try and sidestep what he views as a romantic gesture. "It seems fitting that she should handle that discussion."

"Sure." He smirks. "Keep telling yourself that. You're a good husband, Graham, whether you want to admit it or not."

I'm a shitty husband.

I'll admit that.

I'm paying my wife to be here. If that's not as fucked up as a marriage can get, I sure as hell don't know what is.

———

I CLOSE the doors to the guestroom softly before turning to make my way toward the small bedroom I'm currently staying in.

I don't make it a few feet before I notice light filtering from a doorway on my left.

I quicken my steps. Old habits die hard, and I've never shaken the one that sends me to the light switch when leaving a room. In this case, I'm picking up Lloyd's slack since it seems that he forgot to turn off the lights in the library.

Just as I step inside the doorway to reach for the switch, I notice movement on the other side of the room.

It's my wife with her back to me.

She's on her tiptoes with that black dress she's been wearing all night swinging on her hips.

I could watch this for hours.

I should walk over and offer to help her retrieve the book she's reaching for, but I don't.

I stare.

Suddenly, and without any fucking warning, she spins around to face me.

Jesus. My cock can't take much more of this.

Her glorious tits are straining against the fabric of the dress since it shifted, likely from her trying to grab a book that's well out of her reach.

"Graham." My name comes out of her wrapped in an almost moan.

It's probably a goddamn groan of exasperation, but in my mind, it's being filed away for eternity as a fucking moan.

"Trina," I shoot her name at her with a smile. "What are you doing?"

It's rhetorical and meant to keep her standing there looking like the dream she is.

It works.

She heaves a heavy sigh. "I wanted a book, but I'm not tall enough to reach it."

I've never swooped in to be the hero for any woman, but then again, I've never been married before.

I take wide steps until I'm right in front of her.

That sends her back a touch on her bare feet. "It's that novel up there."

There are thousands of books lining the wooden shelves in this room. The former owner had a thing for books and no will to speak of, so I inherited them when I bought the apartment.

One day I'll get around to donating them all to a worthy cause. That can't happen until Lloyd is gone. He loves this library.

I inch closer to her. "Which novel?"

"That one," she says without movement.

"I can't read… minds, Trina."

The slight hesitation between my words sends a small grin to her lips. "I'll say you can't."

She tries to turn to face the bookshelf, but I stop her by grabbing hold of her forearm. "What does that mean?"

I feel a shiver race through her, but it's warm, way too fucking warm in here for her body to react that way. It's because of my touch. It has to be.

"You know what it means," she whispers.

I don't bother whispering back because Lloyd had so much wine that he's likely passed out by now. Besides, the guestroom is too far from here for voices to carry. "I don't. Tell me."

She shifts on her feet, tugging against my touch, but there's no fight in her. She's not putting any effort into trying to break free of my grasp. "You're not the most perceptive man in the world."

I toss my head back and let out a deep laugh. "What the fuck?"

She digs in. I feel it in the way her arm flexes. "You aren't good at reading between the lines. You miss signals all the time."

"What signals?" I bite the words out because my cock, once again, is waging war with me.

I want this woman more than I've wanted anyone in my life.

"I can't list them all," she says with a hint of fake exasperation edging her tone.

"List one," I demand with a smirk.

She laughs that off with a nervous uneven giggle.

I glance down to catch sight of the top of her full breasts. I drag my gaze back up just in time to see the tremor of my wife's bottom lip as she slicks her tongue over it.

"You want me to kiss you, Trina."

Her chin rises slightly. "Why would you say that?"

"Because I'm perceptive," I say, keeping my eyes trained on her face. "Don't deny it, Mrs. Locke. You want to kiss me just as badly as I want to kiss you."

"You want to kiss…"

I swallow her last word when I press my lips to my wife's for a kiss that I know will leave me a different man. I hope it leaves my wife with an aching need for more.

CHAPTER TWENTY-THREE

T‍RINA

I GIVE in to my body's need and tangle my hands in my husband's hair.

That lures a soft groan from him as he deepens the kiss.

I fight to keep in a moan, but I'm lost to it as soon as I feel his hand on my back.

It trails down until it's on the top of my ass.

His lips leave mine just long enough for him to bite my name out in a strangled whisper. "Trina."

I don't need him to say anything else. I feel it. I sense what he wants because it's what I'm craving too.

I want him to touch me.

"Graham, please." It's a plea that I can't contain.

I have never wanted a man more than I want him.

My breath hitches when his hand slides under the skirt of my dress.

"Lace," he grits out as soon as his fingertips find my panties. "What color?"

"Red." I somehow manage to get the word out before his lips are on mine again.

Our tongues dance against each other. The exploration is much more tentative than his hand. I can feel it gliding across my ass. Two fingers dip under the thin strip of lace covering my hip.

"I'm going to ruin these," he warns before he rips the panties apart with a yank of his hand.

I hold in another moan and instead let two words out. "Not here."

"Here," he insists just as his fingers burn a hot path over my skin.

I kiss him deeper, wanting to taste him. He's a heady mix of the wine we had at dinner and something minty. It's intoxicating. My mind clouds with images of him fucking me here on the floor like two people too desperate to have the will to walk down a hallway and hide their desire behind a door.

As his fingertips trace a path over my pussy, a scream charges through me.

He catches it with a kiss so decadent that I drop one of my hands to the front of his pants.

I curve a palm around his erection. He's thick and so hard that I want to drop to my knees and circle my lips around his shaft.

"Want to fuck you," he grits out with my bottom lip between his teeth.

I fumble with one hand to undo his belt.

Common sense doesn't have a part in this. Pure need is driving every motion of my body and every sound falling from me.

I tense when his finger finds my clit.

The hum that falls from his lips onto mine is enough to send my hips forward.

I ache for his touch and the promise of the pleasure, even though I fear the aftermath.

If he fucks me it changes everything.

I chase that thought away as I push closer, tempting him to take more. I want more. I want both of his hands on me. I want that mouth on my pussy, and I need that cock that's still pressing against my palm.

A sharp noise stops us both.

Our lips part in slow motion, with an ache settling over mine almost immediately.

I lock eyes with my husband.

He doesn't break our gaze even when the sound fills the silence again.

It's a chime. A lure that is meant to take his attention away from me, but he ignores it.

I almost fall back into assistant mode and remind him to check his phone, but I want to be more important than whoever is trying to reach him.

He glances at my mouth, and I know what he's thinking before the words leave his lips because they are primed on mine.

"I want my cock in your pretty little mouth."

The words are so bold and uninhibited that I can feel desire pooling between my legs. He must feel it too, because he groans his approval as his fingers slide through my wetness.

"You're so ready for me," he says hoarsely. "You want my cock."

I squeeze it through the rough fabric of his pants. "Only as badly as you want me."

His eyes flare open. They're wide with the same yearning I feel inside. "I'm going to fuck you here. Now, Trina."

I hear it as a promise and not a threat.

I'm in such desperate need for his touch that I'd let him parade me naked down Broadway if I knew his cock was my reward.

His phone sounds once again, interrupting our need-fest with another chime.

"Goddammit," he mutters under his breath with his lips pressed against mine.

I feel him slipping from greedy husband to devoted CEO, so I part my feet. It's just enough to serve as a silent invitation to take more from me.

"Jesus," he whispers when two of his fingers slide into my channel. "You're tight. You're so fucking tight."

I close my eyes, not wanting him to see how badly I need him.

He heaves out a guttural groan just as his phone rings.

The sound cuts through the moment like a jagged knife.

He fingers me in a slow pace as his thumb hones in on my clit.

From beneath hooded eyelids, I watch him. His gaze is set to my face as his fingers go deeper. Each thrust into me is sure and skilled.

I close in on my orgasm with sharp, short jerks of my hips as he leisurely uses his fingers to take me there.

The phone quiets, but within the time it takes to catch my next breath, it starts ringing again.

With his eyes pinned to mine, his finger finds that spot inside of me that sends me into an immediate, intense climax.

I reach down to grab his hand. I ride it through the crest, and as I hold in a moan that could wake the dead, he takes my mouth in a deep, lush kiss.

As soon as our lips part, he dips his other hand into his pocket to retrieve his phone. He answers the call. "Locke."

Trying to find my bearings, I stumble back a step.

Graham bends down, scoops up my torn panties from the floor, and leaves me a panting mess as he heads out of the room, telling someone else that he'll see them right away.

CHAPTER TWENTY-FOUR

GRAHAM

I'M A BASTARD.

I see no reason to sugarcoat the truth. I never have.

With my fingers still inside of my wife, I answered my phone.

In the hours since it happened, I've managed to half-convince myself it was for self-preservation. I was feeling something when I watched her orgasm.

It wasn't the same empty satisfaction I always feel when I'm with a woman.

It doesn't matter how many times I've been told that the sex was great or someone wants more, it's always the same hollow void that is never filled by a lover's words of appreciation.

Tonight was different.

I watched Trina's face as she gave in to her body's raw need. I felt her pussy clench around my fingers as I lured her closer to an orgasm.

I could tell it wouldn't take long even though I wanted, in some abstract selfish, and fucked up way, for it to take forever.

I wanted to freeze time with Trina on the precipice of her climax so I could cement the memory of the way she looked in my mind for eternity.

When the phone rang for a second time, I saw it as a coward's escape from the emotions that had fought their way to the surface inside of me.

I felt connected to my wife as we shared that moment.

I wanted to drop to my knees, press my mouth to her pussy, and taste every drop of her need.

But I didn't.

I answered the goddamn phone.

I listened as a friend invited me for a drink while I watched in wonder as the most beautiful woman who has ever drawn a breath came down from the high of an orgasm.

I felt it.

I almost lost it as her pussy gripped my fingers like a velvety soft vice.

Then I took her ripped panties and raced out of my penthouse so I could get a lungful of air that didn't taste or feel like her.

I haven't managed to find that yet.

She's all around me even as I sit in this almost vacant bar and listen to a man I've known for more than a decade comment on a story that is considered breaking news in the world of finance. I consider it a waste of my time because what's bad news today is yesterday's news by the time I wake up tomorrow.

"Graham." He snaps his fingers near my ear. "Are you listening to me?"

"Bane," I say his name in a pissy tone. "I'm sitting here,

aren't I?"

His blue-eyed gaze drops to my left hand and the silver band that circles my finger. "You're thinking about your wife."

The accusation is so marred in suppressed sarcasm that I huff out a laugh. "What if I am?"

He studies me, likely trying to determine if I'm serious or not.

He finally abandons that thought with a shake of his head. That's followed by a shove of his hand through his black hair.

It's not a gesture of frustration as it is when I do it. Kavan Bane never shows annoyance or weakness. He's a powerhouse. A man who has been dragged through life's gutter and managed to crawl out without giving a shit about anyone or anything.

Yet, I consider him a friend and a close one at that.

"Is it still a fake marriage?"

Kavan was part of the toast to my wife on our wedding night. I met him, Harrison Keene, and Sean Wells in the private dining room of a French restaurant on Tenth Avenue.

It was one of our monthly dinners.

Those started shortly after we graduated from the boarding school we all attended. College sent us in different directions, but we made a point of getting together whenever we could.

Since then, all of our lives have changed in remarkable and torturous ways.

We toasted to my sham of a marriage after I exchanged vows with Trina at the courthouse.

My three friends didn't voice their approval or any disappointment. They understand the reason I put a ring on my assistant's finger.

After the toast, I thought the subject was a moot point.

"Screw you," I toss out the phrase that has served me well since I was a fifteen-year-old kid with long bangs.

"Mature," Kavan counters the same way he always has.

I take a mouthful of the drink in my hand, mentally searching for a way to shift the discussion to anything but my wife.

"I appreciate this," he goes on, "I'm not talking about the drink."

I paid the tab as I often do when we sit side-by-side in this place. I still don't know how it always turns out that way. Kavan is worth a hell of a lot more than I am.

"I know," I say quietly. "I know."

I know that sometimes he needs to sit and talk about nothing with someone who has witnessed everything he's been through.

He taps the top of the bar with his fist. "I'm going home. Where are you headed?"

On another night, it might be to the club a few blocks over to find a woman willing to take me to her place for a fuck, but not tonight.

"Home too," I answer before I finish what's left in my glass. "I have a full day tomorrow."

That's a lie, but Kavan won't know. I'm notorious for going into the office on Sundays. I've always spent more time there than anywhere.

Sliding to his feet, he looks me dead in the eye. "There's no shame in falling in love with your wife, Locke."

I laugh that off in a low chuckle. "Not going to happen."

I tell myself that over and over again as he exits the bar and disappears out of view.

I may have felt a connection to my wife tonight that transcended what we agreed to, but love isn't in the cards for me, especially not with Miss Shaw.

CHAPTER TWENTY-FIVE

Trina

SUNDAYS ARE A DAY OF GRACE.

My mom would tell us that when we were kids, right before she handed us a list of chores that needed to be tended to in our home or at the bakery.

I was always the first to volunteer to wash the floor.

It was a mindless job that never required much effort on my part other than handling a string mop and a large pail of soapy water.

Since I've lived away from home, I've used Sundays to recharge.

I'm doing that today, but it's not because I want a reset. It's because I need an escape.

I couldn't sleep after coming on my boss's hand right before he answered his phone.

He took a goddamn call while his fingers were inside of me. It was mere seconds after he honed in on that spot that no man has ever found before.

At least not with me.

It wasn't even a treasure hunt for Locke. He didn't need a map. He instinctively knew how to curl one of his fingers in just the right way to send me into an earth-shattering orgasm.

He did that and then seamlessly answered his phone before rushing off to meet someone else.

I didn't even get a *goodbye*, or *that was fun*.

It felt like he penciled in ten minutes to finger fuck me before he continued with his night.

If the dictionary is looking for an image to accompany the definition of humiliation, they could have taken a picture of me last night when I went to bed.

I was defeated.

Embarrassed, and yes, I was mad.

Mad at my husband for answering the phone but also angry with myself for letting my guard down.

I know better than to trust him.

I handle his business affairs. He's as cutthroat as they come. Less than two weeks ago he axed a long-time employee. When I asked why he said it was because they hadn't lived up to the Abdons ideal.

He didn't live up to the Trina Shaw ideal last night, so this fake marriage is officially in separation mode until at least midnight tonight.

I left Mr. Abdon a note on the kitchen counter this morning telling him that I had something to take care of today but would see him tomorrow after work.

I didn't leave anything for Graham because he deserves nothing from me.

I'm going to spend today back in my simple world with the people who mean the most to me.

Before I do that, I slip the wedding rings from my finger. Instead of shoving them into the pocket of my jeans, I tuck them into a compartment within my purse. I zip it up to secure them in place.

I may not place any emotional value on them, but monetarily they are worth a lot, and once my marriage has come to an end, I'm giving them both back to Mr. Locke.

Maybe one day if he finds a woman willing to marry him for the right reasons, he can give her Mr. Abdon's late wife's wedding band.

I doubt a woman exists who would fall in love with him, but miracles happen on a daily basis in New York City, so there's a slim chance.

As for me, I plan on letting fate lead me to a man I'm meant to marry. By that, I mean a man who won't take a call when I'm riding his hand to a mind-numbing orgasm.

With a lingering sting still gnawing at me after what transpired last night, I tug open the door to my family's bakery.

I'm going to spend the day here helping my mom since I know she's making a batch of cinnamon buns.

"Trina is here!" Clara screams at no one in particular.

I can't mask the smile that takes over my lips.

This is home.

It doesn't matter where I go to sleep at night because this sugar-scented brick-faced building in Brooklyn has always felt like my home.

I did my homework in a back room here. I learned how to bake chocolate cake and almond cookies in the industrial kitchen, and I watched a few of my older siblings fall in love here.

My sister, Falon, pops into view from the kitchen. "Triny!"

I lunge myself at her.

Her arms offer me a sense of comfort I've never found with anyone else.

She's only older than me by a few years, but I've always looked to her for guidance and advice.

"Fal," I whisper her name as I relish the embrace. "When did you get back to town?"

"Last night," she says as she pushes back to look me over. "I've missed you."

I'd say the same, but I don't think I can get the words past the lump in my throat. I've never kept secrets from Falon, but I have to now. I can't tell her that I married my boss for a short stint to fuel the dreams of a dying man.

It sounds great in logic, but the situation itself is beyond illogical.

It's complicated, and that doesn't scratch the surface of what happened between Graham and me last night.

"What's new in your world?" she asks with a tilt of her head. That sends her brown curls bouncing around her shoulders. "Is there anything I should know about?"

"You should know that I'm craving a cinnamon bun." I laugh. "I'm here to help make them."

"I'm on board for that." She wiggles her left hand in the air. "I need to take off my wedding rings first. Remember the time I lost them in the croissant dough?"

I watch silently as she slips the rings that hold so much meaning to her off her finger. Within the hour, they'll be back where they belong.

They're a symbol of her deep and unbreakable bond with her husband, Asher. Mine are nothing but a representation of the depth of my deception and the knowledge that I chose to marry a man who walked away from me last night during one of the most vulnerable moments of my life.

CHAPTER TWENTY-SIX

GRAHAM

"YOU'RE HERE EARLY," I comment to my wife as I pass her desk en route to my office.

Trina glances in my direction. "I have a busy day."

It's nothing compared to mine.

My assistant stacked meeting upon meeting into my calendar for today. Most of those magically appeared during the past two hours.

She's spent her time making sure that I won't be hanging out here today.

She avoided me with masterful grace yesterday, even going so far as to arrange a catered dinner for Lloyd and me last night.

Bette was at the helm of that. I have no fucking idea why Trina chose to recruit Lloyd's spy to serve an under-seasoned halibut dinner to us, but Lloyd cleaned his plate like it was his last meal.

Thankfully, it wasn't.

He was up at the crack of dawn this morning trying to hunt down my wife to thank her for her thoughtfulness. She'd already left for work.

If I hadn't heard her moving around in my bedroom last night, I would have assumed that she had one foot out of the door of our marriage, but she was there padding around on the hardwood floors before I noticed the exact moment she shut off the lights to go to bed.

My gaze was pinned to the small sliver of light that crept under the door that separated the two of us.

I debated whether or not to let myself into my bedroom to talk to her about what happened in the library the other night.

For once, I acted like the gentleman Lloyd thinks I am, and I stayed put.

I stop before I reach my office door. "We should talk."

Trina's gaze darts to my face. "You don't have time to talk."

She has a good point.

According to the jam-packed schedule she sent me via email, I have precisely twenty-two minutes until I need to be in a meeting at an office in midtown.

"I'll make the time. After all, it's what I do best." I smirk because old habits die-hard, and watch jokes along with puns that involve time are an integral part of working for Lloyd Abdon.

Her lips stay in place. There's no smile, but at the same time, she's not frowning.

I'll take that as a win.

"We don't need to talk," she tosses that at me with a final gaze before she diverts her attention to her laptop screen.

"We do," I counter.

Her arms cross over the light blue blouse she's wearing. "About?"

Trina Shaw is far too intelligent to think I'll fall for this ploy. "Trina."

"Graham," she says my name in the middle of one of those groan moan things that make me instantly hard.

"My office," I spit both words out through clenched teeth.

"Is over there," she snaps back with a finger wagging in the air toward my open office door.

I glance at it for some goddamn reason.

She seems to take some pleasure in that because when I look back at her, my wife is almost smiling.

I fight off one of my own. "This won't take long, Trina."

"What won't take long?"

That question doesn't come from my wife's perfect lips. The voice is too throaty.

I close my eyes because I deserve all of this.

I took off like a selfish asshole after fingering Trina to an orgasm. I deserve to suffer.

"Kay!" Trina bounces to her feet. "You're here."

"In the flesh." Kay spins to show off the floral print dress she's wearing. "You said it was important, so I came in early."

I turn to face the watch designer. "How much of our conversation did you overhear, Kay?"

She looks me over before her gaze settles on my left hand. "Oh my god! Are you married? Who the hell married you?"

Her hand flies up to cover her mouth after that last question.

Trina bows her head. I suspect it's to bite back laughter.

"The most exquisite woman I've ever met did."

That instantly draws my wife's gaze to my face. She studies me, which suits me fine because I can't take my eyes off of her.

"Do I know her?" Kay presses for more. "What's her name?"

"I'm her," Trina whispers.

"What?" Kay shouts. "You didn't say you're her, did you, Trina?"

Trina answers that with a wiggle of the fingers of her left hand in the air. The overhead lights bounce off the diamond. "I did. I'm Graham's wife."

It's the first time I've heard those words, and they strike something inside of me that reaches deeper than anything I've ever felt before.

"Is this real?" Kay screeches. "Is today April first? This has to be a joke. It can't be real."

I lock eyes with Trina and answer for myself since I can't speak for her. "It's real, Kay. Trina agreed to be my wife, and I consider myself an incredibly lucky man."

CHAPTER TWENTY-SEVEN

Trina

GRAHAM SURPRISED ME JUST NOW.

Actually, it goes far beyond that. He shocked me into utter silence when he declared to Kay that he married the most exquisite woman he's ever met.

I couldn't tell if he was being sincere or if he was trying to sell our situation to Kay. I know she's known Lloyd for decades, so it wouldn't be beyond the scope of reason to assume that Graham was trying to convince Kay that our marriage is real.

For a half-second, after hearing that, I semi believed him.

"When did this wedding take place?" Kay's gaze volleys between Graham and me. "It must have been recently because you weren't wearing that rock the last time I saw you, Trina."

"It wasn't soon enough," Graham answers.

Kay's hands jump to the center of her chest. "How romantic is he?"

On a scale of one to ten, I'd rate him a negative one, but I just smile so Graham can continue his string of lies.

"Lloyd has to be over the moon." Kay bounces in her shoes. "He always wanted Graham to find the perfect woman, and it looks to me like he did."

Considering the source, I take that as a compliment.

"Trina has more good news to share," Graham effortlessly segues into the reason I called Kay in. "I have a meeting I need to get to."

I glance in his direction to find him staring at me. "I'll speak to you later."

Kay laughs. "I'm not going to tell anyone if you kiss each other goodbye."

Before Graham can sweep me up into a kiss that rivals the one from the other night, I move to plant a soft one on his cheek.

"You should go," I whisper. "You don't want to be late."

He stares into my eyes. "I'll be back before you know it, Mrs. Locke."

"That's adorable." Kay busts out an ear-to-ear grin. "I'm kicking myself for not seeing this before today."

"For not seeing what?" Graham questions.

"How in love you two are." She bats her eyelashes. "I can't wait to spread the good news."

Great.

Before the day is over, everyone who works for Abdons will know that I married my boss.

"GOOD NEWS TRAVELS FAST." Lloyd beams as I step off the elevator into Graham's penthouse just before six.

I don't have to ask what that's about.

A steady stream of my co-workers stopped by my office today with their well wishes for a long and happy marriage. Most of those were accompanied by looks of confusion, but I simply nodded over and over again.

Deceiving the people I have to see on a daily basis isn't something I want to do, but I'm so deep into this that I don't have a choice at this point.

"Kay told me how thrilled she is by the news about her design, and," Lloyd pauses to draw out the moment before he goes on, "your marriage!"

I smile. "She was really happy about her design being chosen."

Lloyd purses his lips. "I happen to think that her design will catch on like wildfire. I'm sensing our biggest sales numbers are on the horizon when that design launches."

Graham would disagree, but I'm on the Kay train. I believe a throwback to a traditionally designed watch is the right move for Abdons.

Lloyd takes a step back to study me. "You think I made the right call about that, don't you, Trina? I see you're a fan of our timeless designs."

I glance at the watch on my wrist. "Why mess with elegance?"

"I agree," says a deep voice from behind me.

I glance over my shoulder to see my husband approaching us. *What the hell?*

I left the office before him. He came back from his tenth meeting of the day thirty minutes ago and slammed his office door shut. I used the opportunity to sneak out.

Since I came straight here from work, he either has a twin, or there's a secret elevator he boarded that brought him up here before me.

"My driver brought me home," he answers my unspoken question. "You left early, so I didn't have a chance to tell you that he was waiting by the curb in front of the building for us."

I saw the car.

I marched right past it on my way to the subway because I assumed the driver was taking a much-needed break after chauffeuring Graham around Manhattan all day.

"I like the subway," I say before I shift my focus back to Lloyd.

"You and me both." Lloyd sighs. "The subway sets the pulse of this city. You can step on there and take stock of those around you. I've made more friends riding the train than I have at any country club or business meeting."

I've never been to a country club, and my business meetings are typically with the people I work with. I already consider them my friends.

"I make a point of avoiding the subway," Graham says as he moves to stand next to Lloyd. "Besides, I already have all the friends I need."

Lloyd's hand jumps to my husband's shoulder. "Those friendships will withstand the test of time, Bull. The Buck boys bond is a strong one."

Before I can question what that's about, Graham shifts the subject to something that has nothing to do with him. "Since Lloyd had a craving for pizza that's on the menu for dinner. I've arranged for delivery at seven."

"I can't wait." Lloyd rubs his stomach through the white button-down shirt he's wearing. "You two are spoiling me. Why are you so good to me?"

I bow my head because we're far from good to him. We're liars who are pretending to be something we're not.

"I'm going to take a shower before dinner," I say. "I'll be back out before the pizza gets here."

Graham catches my eye. "I ordered a pepperoni and mushroom pizza with extra cheese for you."

"You what?" I don't try to mask the surprise in my tone.

"It's your favorite from the place in Brooklyn that you like."

I stare at his lips as I struggle to comprehend what he said. How the hell can he know any of that?

Now is not the time to play twenty questions with him, so I manage a small smile. "Thank you."

"Anything to make you happy," he whispers before he leans forward to brush his lips over my cheek.

CHAPTER TWENTY-EIGHT

GRAHAM

FINALLY, all of those long-winded minutes to our staff meetings came in handy.

I carted a stack of them home with me last week, and since then, I've been reading them over each night before I fall asleep.

It's not because I find shoptalk fascinating.

That's a lie.

I'm always willing to reread anything about profits rising, but that hasn't been my focus since I started combing through the documents Trina judicially types up after every staff meeting.

I honed in on the small talk that typically takes place before the meetings officially start.

I'm often running late, so my assistant will start her note taking as soon as everyone else is present.

So far, reading through the minutes, I've discovered that Trina's birthday is in May. Her favorite flowers are white chrysanthemums, she likes her coffee with cream and sugar, and the pepperoni and mushroom pizza from a small restaurant in Brooklyn is her favorite.

I intend to continue my discovery mission until I've learned everything I can about my bride.

"You caught her by surprise, Bull."

I glance to where Lloyd has settled on one of the couches in my living room. "Caught who by surprise?"

With a slight shake of his head, he chuckles. "Your wife, of course."

I wasn't sure if he noticed the shocked look on Trina's face when I mentioned the pizza, but I should know better. Lloyd notices *everything*.

"Those little things make all the difference," he points out as he drapes his arm over the back of the couch. "Every year on our anniversary, I'd surprise Sela with a gift that she wasn't expecting."

I make my way closer to him. "I bet she loved that."

Sela Abdon was a saint.

She helped Lloyd build their company from the ground up, and during her last days, she held his hand as he wept over the loss of their life together.

I admit, watching them say their final goodbyes tore me to shreds.

I was outside the hospital room as she took her last breath. When Lloyd walked out, all I saw was a broken man.

I still see that now.

"She loved me," he says quietly. "I loved her."

I take a seat in a chair across from him. "What you two had was rare, Lloyd."

His fingers skim over his cheek, chasing away a single tear. "I know it. I see the same connection between Trina and you."

What he sees is a commitment to make his final wish a reality.

Trina is pissed at me for bailing on her right after she came on my hand in the library. I can't blame her. It was a dick move. Pizza won't make up for it, but since I've never tried to mend anything between a woman and me, I'm hoping food is a solid first step.

I shift the subject because lying to the man who gave me a second chance at life isn't on my agenda for tonight.

The guilt gnawing at my gut since I married my assistant is only burrowing a deeper hole with every passing hour.

"I've done some research on cardiac specialists," I say, wading into the water that Lloyd warned me to stay out of. "I can pull a few strings and get you an appointment with one early next week."

His eyes lock on mine. "I told you not to worry about it."

Surrendering to the inevitable in this case isn't easy for me.

I want the old man to be here to celebrate the holidays with me. I want to see the smile on his face at the lighting of the enormous Christmas tree at Rockefeller Center. I want to build more memories that mirror the ones I already hold close.

And, I want my wife to be part of that.

Surely, if Lloyd lives beyond the next three months, Trina will agree to prolong our arrangement.

I'll take an extra week or two, or a month or six. I want more of this. I want his wisdom and more time with the extraordinary woman who has made him happier than he's been since Sela passed two years ago.

"Do this for me, Lloyd." The words sound foreign coming from me.

I've never asked a favor of him because he's always

anticipated everything I've needed, even when I disagreed with what he believed was best for me.

Leaning forward to rest his elbows on his knees, he sighs. "My heart is running out of steam, Graham. I've accepted my fate. I need you to do the same. Do it *for me*."

He stresses the last two words as if he's asking a simple favor of me.

He's requesting the impossible, so I cast my gaze down.

I can't agree to that. I'll keep pushing for him to see another doctor. Hell, if I have to, I'll find one who will make a house call.

Losing him will break me. It will crush Trina too, so I'll do whatever it takes to keep him alive for as long as possible.

CHAPTER TWENTY-NINE

Trina

I'm impressed and puzzled by the fact that Graham knew about my favorite pizza and where to order it. I first discovered this pizza when I was with my sister. Falon told me that our mom clued her into it, so I knew it had to be stellar.

My mom may be the greatest baker alive, but she's also a pizza aficionado. She once told me that she became an expert when she and her closest friend would buy pizza on their lunch breaks in high school.

I look up and study my husband's profile as he talks sales numbers with Lloyd.

I won't ask how he knew about the pizza because I believe I've figured that riddle out. It had to have been either Kay or Cecil.

I shared a pie with Kay for lunch one day, and Cecil helped himself to what was left in the fridge in the break room.

One of them must have mentioned to Graham that this is my all-time favorite.

Lloyd breaks free of Graham's gaze and the work-focused conversation to turn his attention to me. "You're an excellent judge of pizza, Trina. This is delicious."

I take credit for the recommendation by smiling as I chew the final piece of crust left on my plate.

"Your wife has exceptional taste," Lloyd points out to Graham. "In food and men."

I work to swallow past the urge to cough when I hear that.

The man he's referring to is still on my *do-not-fool-around-with-again* list. I haven't forgotten that Graham barged out of the library with my torn panties right after I came.

He didn't even have the decency to hang around and make small talk or pull me in for a standing, weak-in-the-knees cuddle.

He bolted when someone on the other end of the phone registered higher on his importance meter than I did.

I haven't wanted to think about whether it was a woman, but I can't stop wondering.

If it was a woman, I don't want to know because I'd feel even more humiliated than I already do.

"She also has impeccable taste in martinis," Graham adds. "She's particularly fond of the ones from the bar across the street."

That's a stretch.

I had one in a hurry when we were avoiding Bette, the chef who wants to be a spy.

I tilt my head and wait for whatever is going to drop from my husband's lips next.

He doesn't say anything.

Lloyd beats him to the punch. "Why don't you two go

across the street and have a drink? It's the perfect way to unwind for the day. I'll read a book and hit the hay soon."

"I'm tired," I say quietly. "I was thinking of hitting the hay too."

More precisely, I was daydreaming about crawling into the bed I've been sleeping like a baby in. It feels like a cloud.

I checked the tag on the mattress because I'm considering buying one just like it after my divorce.

Even though I know the end of this marriage is inevitable, my stomach still knots at the thought of signing the divorce documents.

"Sela and I enjoyed our after dinner drinks." His gaze floats upward. "Whenever I go out for a drink now, I order one for her. It brings me comfort to see it sitting there."

"Come with us," I say, reaching over to cover his hand with mine. "Come for a drink. You can tell me more about Sela."

"Sela would tell me to give the newlyweds a chance to make memories of their own, so you two go ahead. Toast to her for me."

I glance at my husband to see a slight smile on his face.

He catches my eye before he looks at Mr. Abdon. "We'll do that, but we'll also raise our glasses to you, Lloyd. If it weren't for you, I never would have met my wife."

I POP an olive into my mouth and narrow my gaze as I watch Graham sip from a glass of sparkling water.

He opted not to order anything stronger, which made me wonder why I had.

I ordered first, but then, he waited a few seconds before he told the server to bring him a glass of water.

She asked if he preferred a specific brand or whether he wanted sparkling or plain. He chuckled and told her to surprise him.

Judging by the bubbles and the lemon wedge propped on the rim of his glass, I suspect she chose the most expensive brand of water.

"There's a question swirling in that brilliant brain of yours." Graham grins. "Spit it out, Trina."

Shaking my head, I smile. "Is it that obvious?"

"The corners of your eyes crinkle when you're inquisitive," he points out. "Your left brow perks the slightest bit right before you ask a question."

That can't be accurate.

I have a spectacular poker face.

At least I think I do.

"I have a couple of questions," I admit.

He curls his fingers as if he's luring me toward him. "Shoot them my way."

"What's a Buck boy?" I work to hold in a giggle. "And why are you one?"

A smirk coasts over his lips. "Those are your two questions?"

"Consider them one since they're closely related." I dart a finger in the air to accentuate my point.

"I went to The Buchanan School." He tilts his head. "That makes me a Buck boy. It's a long-standing tradition to call yourself that, but I try not to whenever possible."

Both of my eyebrows perk. "You went to The Buchanan School? That's upstate, right? It's private and very exclusive."

That's my polite way of saying the yearly tuition costs a fortune.

Gary, one of my brothers, once joked about sending his

son there when he's ready for high school. The problem is that the all-boys school is only for the ultra-rich.

"I did," he answers simply. "What's the second, or I suppose technically it's your third question?"

"What's with the water?" I ask with a sigh. "I almost feel guilty for indulging in this while you play the good guy."

Huffing out a laugh, he shakes his head. "I'm playing the good guy?"

I nod. "You're not drinking on a work night. That makes you a good guy."

"Is that all it takes?" He leans back in his chair. "I would have cut out the scotch years ago if I knew the path to sainthood was at the bottom of a water glass."

"You don't consider yourself a good guy?"

He scrubs at the back of his neck with his palm. "I have my moments."

"Like when you ordered me to marry you," I quip.

His smile widens. "Ordered?"

"Bribed?"

"Persuaded," he settles on that. "I persuaded you to marry me with a hefty payout."

We haven't spoken about the money since our wedding day. I try not to think about it too much because I've struggled with the amount and the guilt that will always be attached to it.

"You persuaded me by confiding in me about Lloyd's condition," I add. "How is he doing?"

He takes another sip of water. "He's stubborn. He won't let me set him up with a specialist here. It's fucking frustrating."

I see the frustration etched in his movements. He fists his hands on the table.

"Maybe he'll change his mind in time," I say before I think it through.

Time is the one thing that Mr. Abdon doesn't have.

Graham shoves a hand through his hair. "Maybe I should have ordered something stronger."

"But you didn't. Why?"

His gaze searches my face. "I want to have a clear head. We need to talk about what happened in the library the other night."

This is what I feared would happen when we crossed the street and walked into this bar for a drink. "We don't need to discuss that. It happened. It won't happen ever again."

Graham's hand is on mine before I have time to react. He lowers his voice as he stares into my eyes. "It damn well will happen again. I want it to. Fuck it, Trina. I want more."

CHAPTER THIRTY

Graham

MY WIFE STARES at her martini as I confess that I want her.

Since she has nothing to say to that, I keep talking, "I know I fucked up."

That brings her gaze to mine. She waits for a full two beats of my heart before she sighs. "Drop it, Graham. It's in the past."

The past.

The fucking past.

I avoid it at all costs, but tonight, I want to dive headfirst into it. I want to right my wrong.

"I shouldn't have left you the way I did," I continue, ignoring the fact that she has clearly stated that she doesn't want to revisit what happened. "I'm sorry, Trina."

She studies me, tilting her head to the left. "I've never heard you apologize to anyone for anything."

Because I try damn hard not to fuck up so profoundly that my actions require an apology.

"I'm sorry," I repeat, so she knows there is weight in the words. "If I could go back in time to change it, I would."

"But we can't go back in time," she points out. "We can only go forward, and we need to do that with the understanding that intimacy is off the table."

Like hell we do.

I crave her. I've tried to convince myself that it started when I touched her body, but it began before that.

Hell, I'm beginning to wonder if I've always wanted her but brushed the need aside because she was strictly my assistant until I put that ring on her finger.

"Are you attracted to me?"

My direct question lures a soft smile to her lips. "I plead the fifth."

I laugh. "I take that as a yes."

"Take it as a non-answer."

Shaking my head, I press on, "I know you're attracted to me."

She takes a large sip of her martini, drawing out the silence sitting between us as I eagerly wait for her to respond.

"You're cocky," she finally spits out. "Your ego is huge."

"You're not saying that's a bad thing, are you?" I ask with a raised brow.

"I'm saying it's a thing," she states simply. "It's the truth."

I nod in agreement. "I'm confident."

She tugs at the lobe of her ear. "It's more than that. You have this air about you…I can't explain it, but it's as though you know your worth, and you don't care what anyone else says about it."

If that's how she views me, I've come a hell of a long way from where I was ten years ago.

I sip from my water glass to give her the chance to continue.

She does. "When we first met, I was surprised by how good-looking you are."

Now, we're getting somewhere.

"You were?" I ask, wanting to keep her on this track because, *yes*, it fucking feeds my already stuffed ego.

"From what Lloyd told me, I had painted this mental picture of you that didn't compare to the real thing."

As tempted as I am to ask what Lloyd said about me, I skip past that because there are far more important matters to discuss.

My wife's attraction to me tops that list.

"Let's just say that I didn't expect that when I arrived to work on my first day." She punctuates the words with a circle of her index finger in front of my face.

I mimic her movement by trailing one of my fingers in the air directed toward her. "That feeling was mutual. I can't say I ever had an assistant who looked like you."

Her hand drops as her eyes widen. "I didn't think you noticed the way I looked."

My head falls back in laughter. "How could I not notice you? You're beautiful, Trina."

Her mouth curves toward a smile. "You think I'm beautiful?"

The question draws another hearty chuckle from deep within me. "Have you looked in a mirror? You're breathtaking."

MY WIFE EXCUSED herself after I told her she was breathtaking. She claimed that she needed to use the ladies' room, but I watched her from the corner of my eye.

She stopped in the corridor right outside the washroom.

I could tell that she was lost in thought.

I've seen it before when a work matter has stolen her focus from everything.

In those moments, the office tower could be burning to the ground, but Trina would have her gaze glued to her laptop screen.

She's still standing in the same spot now, but her eyes are pinned on what looks like a painting on the wall across from where she's standing.

I glance up at the server as she approaches our table.

"Can I get you another glass of water, sir?" she asks softly. "Or perhaps another martini for your wife?"

Hearing her call Trina that brings a grin to my lips. "I think we're both good."

Her gaze trails toward the corridor where Trina is. "You make a beautiful couple. I'm sure people tell you that all the time."

I nod in agreement because we do make a hell of a gorgeous couple, but we're not that. We're boss and employee, and for the time being, fake married.

She wanders toward another table as my gaze trails back to my wife.

Anger hits me like a freight train when I see some random in a gray suit approaching my wife.

It's not the same guy who hit on her the first time we were in here.

This guy is wearing a tailored suit and has an expensive Abdons watch on his wrist that I catch a glimpse of when he reaches out to touch Trina's shoulder.

The fact that my wife is gazing up at him with a broad smile on her face is making me wish, for a split second, that I was him.

Her right hand reaches out to pat his bicep.

He leans down to plant a kiss in the middle of her forehead, and that's it. That's the line for me because I'm up and out of my chair in a flash.

I sprint across the bar toward where the guy is staring at my wife like he's ready to eat her for a late-night snack.

"Do you promise you'll call me?" Trina asks just as I get within earshot of them.

"Scout's honor," the asshole says as he raises a finger in the air.

I'm no boy scout, but I'm reasonably sure that pledge involves three fingers, not one.

It doesn't matter to my wife. She finds it funny as fuck. That's evident in the way she's laughing at this chump.

I stand and stare at the two of them as Trina's laughter subsides. "How is she?"

"How is who?" Those words escape me before I realize I'm speaking aloud.

"Scout," Trina answers with another small laugh. "I was asking how Scout is."

"Who is Scout?" I toss out another question even though the answer to the last one made absolutely no sense to me.

"My sister," the guy charming the hell out of my wife says. "I'm William Knight, and you are?"

I look at Trina before I answer his question. "Married to the woman you can't take your eyes off of."

CHAPTER THIRTY-ONE

TRINA

OH NO.

Oh, big NO with a capital N and a huge O.

I glance at the stunned expression on William's face before I turn to my husband.

"Graham!" I bite out his name from between clenched teeth.

His gaze drops to where I'm hiding my left hand behind my back.

"Trina," he says my name like everything is fine.

It's not.

He just told the brother of one of my oldest and dearest friends that we're married.

If Scout gets wind of this, my entire family will know that I wed my boss.

That can't happen.

"You're married?" William questions with a quirk of his brow. "Did he just say you're married to him, Trina?"

"Who exactly are you?" Graham chooses this second to go all *she's-my-wife-back-off* on William.

"A friend," William answers honestly. "I've known Trina since she was in the first grade."

Graham's gaze volleys between William and me. "You're just friends?"

William adjusts one of his diamond-studded cufflinks. "We're more like family, which is why I'm surprised you're claiming to be married to Trina. I didn't catch your last name, Graham."

He draws Graham's name out slowly.

I jump into the fray because I need to do some major damage control before William starts spreading the news that I tied the knot.

"Graham is my boss," I begin before I draw a deep breath. "It's a complicated situation, William. We're trying to make a man's dying wish come true, so we're married temporarily, but it's in name only."

Graham clears his throat.

"Technically, it's not in name only," I continue at a rapid pace. The words fly out of me in between nervous breaths. "I'm still Trina Shaw."

William crosses his arms. "Did he force you to marry him? Did he coerce you in some way by leveraging your job?"

"What the hell?" Graham mutters.

"No," I answer quickly. "It's not like that."

"What's it like?" William presses.

I'm so deep into this that I see no way out other than the truth. I draw my left hand back into view. "I married Graham because the man who owns Abdons is ill, and we want to make the little bit of time he has left as happy as we can."

William reaches for my hand to study the rings. "It's

admirable, but you couldn't pretend to be engaged? You had to take it to the next level?"

His concern is deeply rooted in our friendship. He's always been like another brother to me. Ever since I met Scout, her two brothers have kept a watchful eye on me.

William is the oldest. He's also the most intuitive.

"It's temporary," I stress. "I haven't told anyone because it's only going to last a few months. Once it's over, and I'm divorced, I plan on telling my family and Scout."

I add his sister's name to that list even though I haven't seen Scout in almost a year. She's been living in London.

He glances at Graham. "Since Trina wouldn't jump into something like this without her eyes wide open, I'm going to assume you're a stand-up guy, Graham."

"He is," I hear myself saying before Graham can respond.

"This isn't my story to tell, Trina, so you don't have to worry that I'm about to race out of here and call Scout to fill her in."

I smile, feeling like I should thank him for reading my mind.

"Besides, this may not end the way you two think it will." William chuckles. "Life rarely goes according to plan."

"This will end exactly the way we planned." I look at Graham for reassurance. "We'll be divorced soon, and this marriage will be nothing but a memory."

William and I both wait for Graham to chime in, but he stands stoically, staring at my face.

"Like I said," William begins before he kisses my forehead again. "Keep an open mind. Life may have another path for you two."

He pats Graham on the shoulder as he brushes past him before he walks away, leaving me convinced that he's wrong.

The path ahead of my husband and me is clear. There's a divorce in our future, and absolutely nothing will change that.

"WE DIDN'T FINISH OUR DISCUSSION." Graham drops that on me as we ride the elevator back up to his penthouse.

I glance to where he's standing next to me. "Because you went all caveman on my friend."

Rubbing his jaw, he lets out a light chuckle. "Like hell I did."

We didn't discuss anything after William left the bar because Graham had to take a call. I knew instantly that it was a work issue because of the tone of his voice.

He slid back into CEO mode without batting an eyelash as I sipped on my martini. As soon as I downed the last drop, he paid the server for our drinks, and we left the bar.

"You put me in an awkward position," I point out as we near our floor. "Please don't announce that we're married anymore."

His gaze searches my face. "I had no idea that you two were friends, Trina. I thought he was hitting on you."

"What if he was?" I ask simply. "What if a hot guy hits on me?"

"You think William is hot? Are you sure you're just friends with him?" His tone suggests he's joking, but his expression says otherwise.

I stomp my foot just as the elevator doors slide open. "You're insufferable."

"That's a new one." He chuckles. "Insufferable."

I bolt out of the elevator ahead of him, knowing that he likely has his gaze pinned to my ass.

"I'm going to bed," I say without glancing back. "It's been a long day."

"I want to talk." Graham's voice comes out in a low growl. "We're not done discussing what happened the other night, Trina."

That spins me around to face him. "Yes, we are."

"We're not."

Crossing my arms over my chest, I tilt my head. "I'm done talking about it."

"So listen to me talk," he says quietly. "Give me ten minutes. You can spare that, can't you, dear?"

I know he used the endearment to try to get me to smile, but I fight it off. "Ten minutes?"

"Ten minutes," he repeats.

I glance at the watch on my wrist. "Your time starts now."

CHAPTER THIRTY-TWO

GRAHAM

NORMALLY, I perform well under pressure, but I'm struggling to gather my thoughts to present them to my wife.

I could take the to-the-point approach and tell her that I want to fuck her, but I suspect that will earn me a slap in the face and a premature divorce.

"Can we do this in the bedroom?" I ask to buy myself more time.

"The bedroom?" she parrots back with a straight face. "You want us to take this to the bedroom?"

This is a conversation about all the things I want to do in the bedroom, so it seems fitting.

"Yes," I answer succinctly and tack on an explanation for good measure. "I don't want Lloyd to stumble into the middle of this conversation."

She thinks about that for a second. "I don't want him to overhear it either."

We finally agree on something.

"Why don't we do it in your study?"

I've thought about her asking that very question, but in my imagination, she was naked with her hand between her legs, readying herself for my cock.

"My study works," I agree because I'm not a man against compromise.

She stands grounded in place. "I don't know where that is."

Of course, she doesn't.

The tricky maze of hallways in this place is hard to master. I got lost twice when I first moved in.

I walked into a storage closet in search of a shower.

The second time, I landed myself in the laundry room when I was looking for my bedroom.

"Follow me," I say with hope.

There's a chance she'll bolt in the other direction and head for my bedroom.

She doesn't.

I hear her heels clicking on the floor behind me as I lead my wife to the one room in this vast apartment that feels like home to me.

"IS THAT YOU?" Trina questions as I shut the door to my study.

I glance over to where she's pointing at a framed photograph that sits on a shelf.

Nodding, I move closer to her. "That's me."

She leans closer to the picture. "How old were you in this?"

I can tell her to the day, to the hour to be more precise, but I go for a general answer. "Sixteen."

Her gaze darts to my face. "You look the same but different."

I sure as hell hope so.

I've got thirteen years on the scruffy kid in the picture.

"Who are these other guys in the picture with you?" She smiles. "Your brothers?"

"Friends."

I leave it at that.

I'm not going to explain who Kavan, Sean, and Harrison are. She'll never meet them. There's no reason to go into any detail about them.

"Are they Buck boys too?" she asks with a hint of a chuckle.

"Yes."

"Are you still friends with them?"

"I am," I answer swiftly.

Chewing on the corner of her bottom lip, she sighs. "Why is it so hard to imagine you as someone's friend?"

I huff out a laugh. "Ouch?"

She doesn't apologize for the question or attempt to backtrack. Instead, she doubles down. "You don't strike me as the type of man who allows other people to get close to him."

That hits so close to home that I drop my gaze to the floor of my study.

"No one has ever called the office for you in a personal capacity," she explains. "I've never booked a lunch or dinner reservation for you and a friend."

I glance up at her. "I handle those myself."

"Right," she says with a curt nod of her chin. "That's how you book reservations for dates too."

It's a statement, not a question, so I see no need to respond to it.

She looks at her watch. "Time is running out."

Holding back a smile, I shake my head. "Time starts now. Your attention was diverted because of that picture."

Shrugging a shoulder, she looks around. "We didn't discuss whether distractions factored into our agreement."

"They do," I insist. "So time starts this second."

She taps the face of her watch with her fingernail. "Go."

"You enjoyed what we did the other night, Trina."

Shaking her head, she laughs lightly. "That's one way to start a discussion."

"I'm not lying," I point out. "You had a good time."

"I had a good orgasm," she corrects me.

I can't fight off a smile. "So we agree on that?"

"It was an orgasm, Graham." She crosses her arms over her chest. "It was a fleeting moment in time. Then it was over, and you left."

"Which was a mistake," I admit for the second time tonight.

"It doesn't matter if it was or not." She rests her hip against the edge of my desk. "It's the past."

I take a step closer to her. "If I hadn't left that night…"

Her hand darts into the air. "But you did, so let's not go down the what-if road. It serves no purpose."

"If I hadn't left that night," I begin again as I close the distance between us with measured steps. "We would have fucked."

Her gaze drops to my lips. "Says who?"

I drag my teeth over my bottom lip. "Says me."

"You're too cocky for your own good."

"Again, I'm not lying, Trina." I stop just inches short of where she is. "I would have taken you to bed and fucked you over and over again."

She retreats half a step. "That would have been an even bigger mistake."

"Why?"

"Why?" she parrots. "We can't have sex."

"Why?" I repeat as I step closer yet.

"It would complicate this." Her hand circles the air between us.

"This is becoming increasingly complicated," I point out. "We are bound to each other for the moment. I say we make the best of it."

Her eyes lock on mine. "There are other women out there, Graham. Judging by what you said, no one turns you down, so why not go find someone else to fuck?"

"I'm not going to fuck anyone else when I'm married to you."

Her eyebrows perk. "You're not?"

"This may be a marriage of convenience, but I won't cross that line," I stress the last word.

"You're not going to sleep with another woman until we're divorced?"

If I have to answer a dozen questions to get my point across, I will. "I'm not going to fuck another woman until we're divorced."

Her gaze drops to my mouth. "I didn't realize that…"

"That I was going to be committed to you in every possible way?"

She nods.

"Let me make this as clear as I can, dear." I toss her a grin. "The only woman I want to fuck is standing in front of me."

"You want me because you can't have anyone else." Her voice is barely more than a whisper.

"I want you because of you," I say. "Because I haven't stopped thinking about how you looked when you came the other night and those sounds you made. And your pussy, Trina. So soft and so fucking tight."

Her hand leaps to my forearm. "Graham, if we…"

"When we," I correct her. "When we fuck it won't change anything."

Her gaze searches my face. "We'll still get divorced as planned?"

"Nothing changes," I say the words like I mean them, even though I know they are laced with a lie.

This marriage has already changed who I am.

"It's just sex," she states clearly.

She can fool herself into thinking that, but after what we experienced the other night, this connection between us far surpasses a physical act.

I nod.

Her hand moves to her forehead. She scrubs it lightly. "I have to think about this."

That's better than a flat out no, so I step aside. "Take all the time you need."

Her lips part slightly as she studies my face. "I will."

I start toward the door, but her hand on my shoulder stops me. "Graham?"

I turn to face her again. "Yes?"

She shakes her head slightly before she lets out a heavy exhale. "I didn't know that you intended to be faithful to me."

I see the way her bottom lip trembles as she waits for my response.

"I may be a shitty boss, but I want to be a good husband. Even if this marriage will be short-lived."

She nods. "Thank you."

I should be the one thanking her for everything she's done for me, but I can't find the words to express the depth of my gratitude. I doubt like hell I ever will.

CHAPTER THIRTY-THREE

Trina

I STEP INTO MY APARTMENT, and suddenly my world feels a whole lot lighter.

A tear falls onto my cheek as I shut the door behind me.

I'm not overwhelmed with emotion at the sight of my one and only houseplant or the view of the building next door out of the living room window.

I'm excited at the prospect of spending my lunch hour here. I started work an hour early today, so that I could bank that time for now. My mom is meeting me here. She spent her morning at the New York Public Library. It's always been her favorite place in Manhattan.

She's going to pick up sandwiches and two lemonades from a deli near the library for us to share.

I already know what the topic of discussion will be. She'll reminisce about when I used to live at home.

Back then, I had so many dreams to fulfill, including meeting a man I'd fall in love with and marry, having kids, and a career path that would eventually see me at the helm of a million or billion dollar company.

Working at Abdons has been the stepping-stone to that, but it's becoming blatantly obvious that I'm going to need to search for a new job once I file for divorce.

I can't imagine walking into the office every day to face my ex-husband.

I move toward the kitchen to grab the small watering can that I keep hidden under the sink.

I fill it with water and relieve the plant of its thirst.

The soil was bone dry which is a clear sign that I need to circle back here every few days instead of once a week.

Just as I set the watering can on the table, there's a soft knock at my door.

My gaze immediately drops to my left hand and the rings.

I slide them off and hide them behind the potted plant.

Another knock sounds, so I smooth my hands over the front of my navy blue skirt and hurry across the floor.

I swing it open with a flourish expecting to see my mom.

Aurora's boyfriend, dressed in his police uniform, greets me instead. "Hey, Trina."

I smile at Eldon. "Hey."

He glances over my shoulder. "Aurora wanted me to open a missing person's file since you haven't been around much. She'll be glad to know you're alive and well."

I let out a light chuckle. "I'm good."

"Do you have a minute?" he asks, adjusting his belt. "I could use a friend to talk to."

I step aside, surprised that he wants to talk.

It's not that we're not friends, but Eldon and I have never had a discussion alone.

I've only ever spent time with him when Aurora has been around.

"Of course," I answer with a smile. "Please, come in."

Before I shut my apartment door, I peer down the hallway, wondering where Aurora is and hoping everything is all right.

ELDON RUNS a hand over his short-cropped brown hair before he takes a bottle of water from me.

He cracks open the lid and swallows more than half of the water in one gulp.

Something isn't right.

His top lip is peppered with sweat, and his left knee has been bouncing since he sat down on my couch.

I take a seat in a chair across from him, crossing my legs before I lean back. "How's Aurora?"

When he glances up at me, I see a glint in his eye. "Beautiful. Perfect. She's great, Trina. She's so great."

That lures a gentle smile to my lips. "I'm glad to hear it."

Nodding, he finishes the water that's left in the bottle. "What's been going on with you?"

I can't exactly tell him the truth. Hell, I can't go anywhere near the truth, so I skip around it. "Work's been busy. I spent some time at the bakery. That's always fun."

"I love the peanut butter cookies from there." A deep belly laugh escapes him. "They're my addiction, but I have to limit myself. I stop in once a week for one."

"For one?" I question with a perk of both brows. "How do you stop at one?"

"It's not easy," he confesses. "But, the job requires me to be in shape, so sugar is off-limits for the most part."

Nodding, I breathe a sigh of relief at the fact that I avoided saying anything about Graham.

I'm semi-surprised that I didn't since I haven't stopped thinking about him since our conversation in his study.

The last few days he's been immersed in work from daybreak to sunset. I viewed that as a gift since I'm still contemplating what he said about us sleeping together.

I want to go to bed with my husband, but I know my heart. Getting emotionally attached to a man I'm divorcing soon isn't the right move for me.

"Can you keep a secret, Trina?"

I almost laugh out loud at Eldon's question. I'm keeping the biggest secret of my life from everyone I care about. It's locked up tight inside of me.

I study him, wondering where this conversation is headed. "I can."

He leans forward, resting his forearms on his thighs. "Aurora's folks are out of town right now. I wanted to talk to them face-to-face, but they're in Indiana for her cousin's wedding. I met the guy once. He was in the city for a night. We invited him to dinner, but he took us out to a restaurant in Tribeca. I admit it was great, but…"

"What is it, Eldon?" I interrupt because that's the most he's ever said to me at one time, and I can tell that he's nervous. "What's going on?"

He scrubs at his forehead while his blue eyes search my face. "Aurora's birthday is coming up."

I'm aware. I've been planning out the perfect gift for her for the past two months. I finally decided on a scarf from the Ella Kara boutique. It's pricey, but I picked it up last month and tucked it away in my closet. I know Aurora will love it.

When I was at the café one day, a woman came in wearing the same scarf. Aurora asked her about it. As soon as the woman left, Aurora made a comment to me about how expensive it must be.

"I know." I smile. "I can't wait to give her my gift."

"That's why I'm here." He taps his shoe against the floor. "I need your help with my gift for her, Trina."

"I'd love to help."

"I got her a ring."

"What?" That pops out in an almost scream. "Are you going to ask her to marry you?"

"Damn right I am. I'm doing it on her birthday." He chuckles. "I want the night to be perfect. I'm planning a surprise party. You're invited, of course. One of her brothers is flying in from Arizona to be there. The other is driving up from Pittsburgh. I can't wait to give her the ring. I think she's going to love it. I hope she'll want to wear it forever."

My gaze drifts to the pot of the houseplant and my rings hidden behind it.

I'm beginning to wonder what it would feel like to wear those rings forever.

His shoulders hunch forward. "I have a small favor to ask. Hell, it's a huge favor, Trina. I'm not one to ask for anything, but this is for Aurora."

"Ask," I insist. "Please, ask me."

"Your brother-in-law is Aurora's absolute favorite singer," he pauses. "Do you think there's a chance that you can get him to sign a birthday card for her? I'll buy the card. Having his autograph would blow her mind. It would be the icing on the cake for the night."

I had no idea Aurora was a huge Asher Foster fan.

"Consider it done." I skim my hands over the front of my skirt. "Don't worry about the card. I'll talk to Asher and handle that."

"Seriously?"

"Seriously." I chuckle. "We're going to make Aurora's birthday one she'll never forget."

"I don't know how to thank you." He smiles, pushing to his feet. "Who would have thought that a random hook-up would lead to a lifetime commitment?"

I stand too and chuckle. "Is that how you met? It was a random hook-up?"

Shaking his head, he laughs. "Aurora never told you that story?"

"No," I answer quietly. "She never mentioned how you two met."

"On an app," he confesses. "It was supposed to be just sex. We agreed to that after our first meet-up. Actually, we agreed it would last through the summer, and then we'd part ways. No harm. No foul since we both were looking for something strictly physical."

"It didn't go as planned," I state the obvious.

He pats the center of his chest. "My heart didn't get the memo not to fall in love with her. That taught me that we don't control everything. Sometimes, you just have to jump in headfirst and see where fate takes you."

CHAPTER THIRTY-FOUR

GRAHAM

MY WIFE HAS GONE ABOVE and beyond this past week when it comes to setting my schedule.

Today she hit a record for the number of meetings she could pack into a nine-hour window. I finished the last thirty minutes ago and decided to walk home.

It wasn't far.

It gave me time to clear my head and think through the discussion I had with Trina the other night.

So far, she hasn't refused my idea to consummate our fake marriage, but she hasn't accepted either. That's mainly because I've barely seen her since work has been my sole focus.

"Mr. Locke!" Eugene, the doorman, rushes at me as soon as I approach the building. He swings the door open with a flourish. "How was your day, sir?"

"Good," I answer brusquely, then consider what my wife would do. "How was your day?"

"Sir?" Eugene asks from behind me as he follows me into the building.

I spin to face him. "How has the day been for you? How's your wife?"

He studies my mouth like he's trying to decode an alien language. "All right on both fronts."

I dip my hand into the front pocket of my suit pants and drag out the bills I deposited in there after I bought lunch for myself.

The three dollar sandwich I picked up at a bodega was a hell of a lot better than the overpriced lunches I typically indulge in.

I glance down at the ten and five dollar bills in my hand. I shove them back in my pocket and reach for my wallet.

I pluck a hundred dollar bill out of that and shove it at Eugene. "This is for you."

His blue eyes travel over my face. "That's far too generous, Mr. Locke."

The gray-haired man has opened the door for me for years now. The majority of that time, I grunted out a greeting to him or ignored him altogether.

Trina would never do that, and if I've learned anything from my wife, it's to treat people with kindness.

I saw it in how she interacted with Bette, and I've heard from Lloyd how kind she's been to the doormen, including Eugene.

"Buy something for your wife." I reach for his hand and tuck the money into his fist.

His hand trembles. "I don't know what to say, sir, other than thank you."

"You're welcome."

"Your beautiful wife arrived home twenty minutes ago," he informs me as he slides the money into the pocket of his jacket. "Mr. Abdon left shortly before that. He told me he was headed to visit one of his favorite places."

I was hoping to have a moment alone with my bride, so this is a gift.

"She's lovely, sir." Eugene smiles. "Mrs. Locke always lights up the lobby when she gets home."

I pat him on the shoulder. "She's an incredible woman. I'm going to head up to see her."

"Enjoy your night." He straightens his jacket. "If you need anything, you know where to find me."

All I need is to hear my wife say she wants me as badly as I want her. Hopefully, that's about to happen.

I EXIT the elevator and am greeted with a sense of silence that weighs on me.

I suddenly wonder if Trina snuck out when Eugene was helping another resident. As I waited for the elevator in the lobby, I noted how he took off to aid an older woman carrying what looked to be her weight in shopping bags.

Eugene scooped them up easily as soon as he opened the lobby door.

"Trina!" I call out into the vastness of this place I call home.

Truthfully, aside from the study, it hasn't felt like home until recently.

I'd attribute that to having Lloyd and Trina as temporary houseguests, but it's more than that.

I've enjoyed the light-hearted banter I've shared during dinners with Lloyd and the unspoken greetings in the kitchen in the mornings between my wife and me.

Lloyd is oblivious to the fact that we haven't spent the night wrapped around each other in my bed.

For the most part, I've spent most nights tossing and turning for hours until I drift off to restless sleep.

That has nothing to do with the comfort level of the mattress or the unfamiliar surroundings.

I've gotten caught up in too many what-if thoughts and moments spent listening to the steady even breaths of my wife as she slept in the next room.

"I'm here." Her voice travels from the east wing. "I was looking for something."

I turn to see her on the approach.

She's wearing ripped jeans and a light blue blouse.

I suppose some would call it a casual look, but it looks elegant and sophisticated on her.

Trina Shaw is a timeless beauty.

She'd steal a man's breath regardless of the century.

"What were you looking for?" I ask.

She moves to stand in front of me. "I found it."

I gaze down at her hands, grateful to see the rings on her finger. "Is it invisible?"

That pulls a laugh from her. Her hand dives into the front pocket of her jeans. She tugs out a diamond stud earring. "It's this. It must have fallen out of my ear in the library the other night."

"I'm glad you found it."

"Me too." She shrugs, dropping the earring back into her pocket. "It's not real, but my sister gave me the earrings as a gift years ago. They have a lot of sentimental value."

I make a mental note to buy her a pair of diamond stud earrings tomorrow.

They may never hold any value to her beyond their purchased worth, but she deserves them. Her beauty will always surpass them, but it will certainly complement the earrings.

"Lloyd went out for a couple of hours." She sighs. "He looked so happy, Graham. Is it wrong to hope that he's feeling better and that he'll…"

"Have more time?" I finish her sentence.

She chews on the corner of her bottom lip. "I'm not a doctor, but he looks better since he arrived in New York. There's more color in his cheeks. He's walking with more bounce in his step. He seems to have more joy."

I've noticed it too and attributed it to my wife.

She's changed my life. How could she not do the same for Lloyd?

"Maybe that's wishful thinking," she continues, "I've gotten to know him better since I started living here, and I don't want him to die."

I watch as her bottom lip trembles.

"I don't want that either," I confess.

"We've made him happy, haven't we?" she whispers. "I mean this marriage, and our living together, it's been good for him, hasn't it?"

Nodding, I take a step closer to her. "It has been good for him."

Her gaze trails over my face stopping at my lips. "I'm getting used to being married to you."

I fight off a smile. "Are you?"

She steps closer to me. "It's not nearly as bad as I thought it would be."

Tossing caution out the goddamn window, I drop a hand to my wife's hip, hoping like hell she doesn't slap me across the face. "It's better than you thought it would be."

Her hand moves to cover mine. "It's going to get even better, Graham."

Not wanting to read between the lines, even though I'm pretty fucking sure she's talking about sex, I act dumb. "How so?"

That earns me a tap on my cheek from her palm. "Don't pretend you don't know exactly what I'm talking about."

I tug her closer so she can feel what she's doing to me. I want her to know that I'm hard as nails just from standing close to her. "You want me to fuck you, Mrs. Locke."

Her eyes meet mine. "If we're stuck with each other for the time being, we might as well make the best of it."

I bark out a laugh. "Frame it however the hell you want to, but you want me, Trina. You can't deny that."

She rests her hand on my shoulder as her lips glide over my cheek toward my ear. "If you're as good in bed as you were in the library, I'm going to enjoy being your wife until we're divorced."

I claim her lips in a soft, lush kiss that leaves her breathless in my arms.

"You'll enjoy it," I whisper as our lips part. "I promise you're going to enjoy it a hell of a lot."

She lets out a faint moan. "Prove it."

CHAPTER THIRTY-FIVE

TRINA

"WE'RE GOING TO USE CONDOMS," I tell him as I slowly unbutton my blouse.

Graham eyes me from where he's standing near the bed. His bed.

We're in his bedroom. I've called it home since the day we married, but this is the first time he's been in here with me for longer than a minute.

He gestures to the nightstand. "I have condoms."

I silently berate myself for not peeking in the nightstand drawers before now.

I never thought to, or maybe my subconscious kept me from doing it out of fear of what I'd find inside.

"Your clothes," I say as I reach the last button. "You're not undressing."

That's not the whole truth.

He's removed his tie and suit jacket. Both landed on a

chair in the corner of this room, but he hasn't taken off his shirt or pants.

He's been watching me with his arms crossed over his chest.

"I will," he whispers. "I don't want to miss a moment of this."

I've never shied away from showing my body to a man. I won't with my husband either.

I slide the blouse from my shoulders and toss it on the same chair where his clothes are.

Before I remove my bra, I undo my jeans. The entire time I keep my gaze on Graham's face.

"You're staring at me," I accuse, suddenly wanting to cut through the intensity of his expression.

"How could I not?" he asks as he stalks toward me. He takes sure and measured steps as his fingers make quick work of the buttons of his shirt.

By the time he's in front of me, his entire chest is exposed. Then the shirt falls to the floor at my feet, granting me my first view of my husband's naked torso.

Damn.

He's all cut muscle and planes of smooth skin.

I reach a tentative hand out to touch him. Trailing a fingertip over his shoulder, I trace a path down his chest to his abs.

Before I realize what's happening, his hands are on the waistband of my jeans.

"You're torturing me, Mrs. Locke," he whispers. "I want you now."

I drop my hands to his belt buckle and answer his plea as I help him lose the rest of his clothes.

"I DIDN'T WANT THIS," he hisses the words out between clenched teeth.

I glance up at him as I trail my tongue over the swollen head of his thick cock. "You're a liar."

A deep belly laugh rolls through him as he yanks on my hair, causing a jolt of pain. "I want to be inside of you."

I slide my mouth over him again, taking him even deeper.

That lures a loud groan from him.

I pull back, letting his cock drop from my lips. "You are inside of me."

That earns me a look that promises that I'll pay later for making him wait to fuck me.

He reaches down to grab hold of my arms, yanking me to my feet.

His lips find mine in a rushed kiss before he twists us around and tosses me onto his bed.

I try to resist when his hands grip my knees. He urges my legs apart.

I feel exposed and vulnerable, but at the same time, wanted in a way I've never felt before.

He gazes down at me as he stands next to the bed. "Jesus, look at you. You're so goddamn beautiful."

I push my cheek into the soft linens of the bed. "Fuck me, Graham."

"I want a taste," he breathes. "I want it so much, but…"

My fingers trace a soft path over my cleft. "You want to fuck me first."

"So badly."

He moves quickly to the nightstand, keeping his gaze pinned to my hand the entire time.

I touch myself. Not caring how it looks to him.

I'm already so close to coming just from watching his

lean muscular frame move and from seeing how aroused he is because of me.

Once he's sheathed, he's on the bed with me. His hands glide down my inner thighs.

"It's been a while for me, " I confess softly. "So please, be…"

"Gentle," he finishes my sentence. "That's asking a lot."

I let out a light laugh. "Be gentle this first time."

He leans forward to kiss my right nipple. "I want to taste every inch of your body, but I need this, Trina. Fuck, do I need to be inside of you."

I urge him forward with a hand on his shoulder. "I need it too."

I gasp when he slides the crown of his cock over my folds. I whimper when he pushes inside, and when he's settled deep, I moan in a voice that I can't recognize.

It's filled with such need and trembling with want, and when he thrusts again, and again, I cry out, knowing that this is better than anything I've experienced before.

He's so deep. When he ups the pace and groans out my name, it reaches a part of me that sends me closer to the edge.

I meet his rhythm as words fall from my lips about needing him to fuck me harder and faster.

He gives me everything I want, and as I reach my climax, he stares into my eyes, revealing a part of him I never knew existed.

I watch him come undone at the same moment as I do. His lips part, and his control, all the control he always carries with him, is stripped away to reveal a man lost in his pleasure, lost completely and wholly to me.

CHAPTER THIRTY-SIX

Graham

THERE IS something achingly poignant about this moment.

I'm in my bed with my wife.

She's lost in thought as her fingers tease her right nipple.

I don't know if she's even aware of what she's doing, but it's slowly killing me inside.

She's incredibly sensual and captivatingly beautiful in a way that has not only made me want her more than I have anyone I've ever met, but I've realized that I'll never feel this way again.

How will another woman ever satisfy me?

It's not about the orgasm, although that was well beyond the scope of anything I've felt before. It was intense, so intense that I thought I'd fucking cry at the emotions that shot through me as I came with her silken pussy wrapped around my cock.

I stare at Trina's profile as she gazes toward the window.

Simply knowing what her favorite pizza is or her preferred flower doesn't seem that important anymore.

I want to know what she sounds like when she comes on my tongue. I want to see her face when she first wakes in the morning, and I want to feel her breath on my cheek when I crawl into bed next to her every night and kiss her senseless before she drifts off in my arms.

"Are you asleep?" she whispers.

I drop my hand over hers to touch her plump nipple. "Wide awake, Mrs. Locke."

She turns to glance at me. "I'm still Trina Shaw."

Legally, but after tonight, she feels like my wife. I want her to be my wife. I don't give a damn about her surname, but I want this – I want more moments like this with us tangled together with rings on our fingers that tell everyone and anyone that I belong to her.

"You are," I agree as I pinch her nipple. "Trina Shaw."

Her gaze drops to my lips. "That was fun."

I inch a brow up. "The fuck was fun?"

"Very." She nods. "It felt different than other times for me."

I don't want to dive into that pool. The thought of another man experiencing anything remotely close to this makes me want to yank my hair out.

"It felt incredible," I whisper. "You're incredible."

She turns to face me, giving me an unobstructed view of her body. "So are you."

I inch my fingers over her stomach. "Are you hungry, Trina? Say no."

A bubble of laughter falls from her swollen lips. "No."

"I am." I move quickly, pushing her legs apart with my shoulders. "I've wanted a taste of you for so long."

Her hands drop to my hair, threading through the strands. "How long? Days?"

"Longer," I say before I glide my tongue over her cleft for my first taste.

My cock hardens even more.

"Weeks?" she whispers through a drawn-out moan.

I part her with my tongue, seeking out her clit. "Longer."

Her back bows when I circle it lightly before sucking it between my lips.

"Mon...months?" she stutters the word out.

I slide a finger inside her as I groan. "Since the day we met."

Her reply is a whimper and a grind of her hips in the air.

I lose everything in that moment. Every thought is gone. Every sensation is focused on only one thing. That's the sweet taste of my wife, and my driving need to make her come.

I WAKE to darkness and an empty spot in the bed next to me.

It takes me a moment to find my bearings.

I glance around, but I don't spot Trina anywhere. A quick look in the direction of the open bathroom door tells me she's left the room.

Panic darts through me.

I'm on my feet in a flash, pulling on my trousers. I zip them up, not bothering with a shirt, before I sprint out of the bedroom.

I stop as soon as I hear her laughter drift down the hallway.

Thank Christ she's still here.

I rest a hand on the center of my chest to feel the pounding beat of my heart. It's racing.

As it begins to slow, I head in the direction of her laughter.

When I finally catch sight of her, my heart starts thundering inside my chest again. This time it's because of the sheer beauty of her.

Her hair is a tangled mess around her face. Her cheeks are blushed pink, and her bottom lip is swollen from the incessant bite of my teeth as I kissed her with a reckless need to be as close to her as I could.

She's wearing jeans and a T-shirt that is emblazoned with the logo from a bakery.

Dobb's Bakery.

"Hey!" she calls out to me as soon as she spots me. "I'm whipping together a little dinner for us."

"Look at you, Graham. It seems someone was napping."

The second voice startles me.

I didn't realize we weren't alone, but Lloyd is perched on a stool next to the kitchen island, watching my wife work some sort of fragrant magic in a skillet.

"It's vegetable stir fry," she offers. "With my secret seasoning. You're going to love this."

Emotions clatter inside me at the way she says it so effortlessly.

I'm going to love this.

I don't know if she's talking about the food or her.

I wipe a hand over my forehead. "I should finish getting dressed."

That draws a deep-seated chuckle from Lloyd. "No need, Bull. I can tell that you two need more alone time. I'm going to call it a night."

"I'm making enough for the three of us," Trina says before stealing a glance at me.

Lloyd pats a hand on the top of the island. "I admit that it smells too delicious to pass up."

I don't blame him for wanting to stick around. Who in their right mind could resist time with my wife and whatever the fuck she's cooking?

Running a hand over my bare stomach, I keep my gaze pinned to Trina. "I'll grab a shirt."

She nods. "We'll be right here waiting for you."

I can't tear my eyes away from her. She looks freshly fucked and happy. She looks as goddamn happy as I feel.

Finally, when she turns her attention back to the pan on the stove, I take off in a sprint down the hallway.

I rush to get dressed because I want every second I can with her. I never want this fake marriage to end.

CHAPTER THIRTY-SEVEN

TRINA

I CURL a finger to lure my husband closer when I spot him returning from walking Lloyd to the guestroom.

Dinner was delicious and fun.

Lloyd ran through story after story about the vacations that he took with his late wife. For the most part, Graham and I laughed at their adventures, but there were moments when sorrow crept into Lloyd's voice.

I reached out to hold his hand as he wept through the retelling of their third honeymoon in Rome. Right after he was finished, he offered to send Graham and me there on our honeymoon.

Neither of us said a word.

I'd love to travel to Italy, but I never considered doing it with my boss.

He's more than that to me now.

The sex was as amazing as I imagined it would be, but it sparked something inside of me.

It might be infatuation or a full-blown hard like, but I'm feeling things for Graham that I haven't felt before.

I need to rein it in since this marriage has an expiry date.

Before I can say a word to Graham, he's got me wrapped in his arms, and his mouth is on mine.

He kisses me deeply. His mouth is demanding but tender at the same time. It's unlike anything I've experienced before. I know after our divorce, I'll never feel it again.

"Come back to bed with me," he whispers as soon as the kiss breaks. "I'm craving you, Trina."

I can tell.

He's hard again.

I feel the length of him pressing against me through the fabric of his pants and the denim of my jeans.

His thumb traces a path over my bottom lip as he gazes into my eyes. "I'm spending the night in bed with you. Every night going forward."

Until this ends.

Those unspoken words sit between us.

I nod because I'll take whatever I can from this. It's not just about faking a marriage anymore. It's about savoring moments like this with him and letting my body feel things it's never felt before.

"I want that," I say breathlessly. "I want you in bed with me."

AS SOON AS I shut the door to Graham's bedroom, his hands are all over me.

He yanks my T-shirt over my head and drops his mouth to my breasts. Feeling the lash of his tongue on my right nipple through the thin silk of my bra sends a shudder through me.

"You like that," he states in a low growl. "You have sensitive nipples."

Unable to find my voice, I nod.

"I'm going to remember that," he whispers as he turns his attention to my other nipple.

The bite of pain when he closes his teeth around it is so intense that I don't register the fact that he's reached behind me with one hand to deftly unclasp my bra.

He slides it from my body, releasing my breasts as he does.

"I'm not going to make it to the bed." He chokes out a half-chuckle, half-groan. "I'm going to fuck you against the wall, Trina. Strip."

I do as I'm told because I want this just as badly as he does.

I want to feel him inside of me again.

My jeans and panties are on the floor before he's back with his hand racing over his sheathed cock.

I stare at his naked body.

All of it is glorious. I had no idea he looked like this under the well-tailored suits he wears.

"You look like you're seeing me for the first time," he says softly.

My gaze drifts up from his cock, to his abs, then his chest, and finally, it settles on his face.

I stare at his chiseled jaw and the way his eyes narrow as he studies me.

"I am," I answer in a whisper. "I feel like I am."

That earns me a kiss so soft and tender that I feel like my knees will buckle on the spot.

"Turn around," he orders as he strokes his cock. "Brace yourself on the wall."

I spin and spread my legs, wanting him inside of me now.

I've been wet since we kissed in the kitchen. I'm on fire with need and a desire so strong that I can't think of anything but being fucked by him.

He takes me quickly, pushing in with one long quick thrust.

I cry out because there's a burst of unexpected pain.

His lips trail over my shoulder as he wraps my hair in his fist. "Forgive me if I'm rough. This is just too fucking good."

His other hand finds my hip, clutching at my flesh.

He fucks me hard.

With each deep thrust, he yanks on my hair until I come so intensely that I call out his name between stuttered breaths.

CHAPTER THIRTY-EIGHT

GRAHAM

"TRINA SHOULD BE at the meeting today," I say to Lloyd over breakfast. "She has a finger on the pulse of what the market wants right now."

My wife's gaze drifts to me. I see surprise in her eyes, but there's something else there. Gratitude.

I know it's for the invitation to join us at the meeting this afternoon for the spring launch campaign. Perhaps there's a small slice of gratitude for the two orgasms she had this morning before she dragged me out of bed.

She woke to find me hovering over her.

I kissed her then before I trailed my lips down her body so I could feast on her pussy.

She wanted to return the favor by taking me in her mouth, but by then, Lloyd was awake and calling my phone, looking for me.

I'll cash in the favor tonight after I surprise her with a

belated wedding gift and something else I sense she's been craving lately.

"I'm all for that." He smiles at my wife. "You've brought new life to Abdons, Trina. Both you and your husband have."

Trina's gaze drops to the rings on her finger. "I'm honored that you trust me to participate in planning the spring campaign. I know how big of a deal that is."

"If your husband trusts you with his heart, how can I not trust you with something like this?" Lloyd replies before he turns his attention back to the bowl of fresh fruit in front of him.

Trina's gaze catches mine, and I see emotion swimming in her blue eyes.

I do trust her with my heart.

I want to say as much, but I don't, because even though this fake marriage has now been consummated, we haven't discussed anything beyond that.

"I'm going to get a newspaper and sit on a bench in the sun for a few hours," Lloyd says as he pushes back from the island so he can stand. "I'll be at the office by two."

Trina's on her feet too. "I'll walk out with you."

"What about you, Bull? Are you heading into work?" Lloyd glances in my direction. "Your tie is crooked."

Before I can reach up to adjust it, my wife is rounding the island headed straight for me.

I drop my hands to her waist as she tugs the knot on my tie loose. Then she skillfully ties it back up before her gaze wanders up to my face. "That's perfect."

"It is," I agree with her even though my words have nothing to do with the goddamn tie around my neck.

This is perfect.

This easy morning routine of coffee and breakfast after a night spent in bed together is utter bliss.

She gazes down at the white blouse and red skirt she's wearing. "How about me? Is everything in place?"

I reach for her left hand and lift it to my lips. I plant a kiss on her palm. "Everything is exactly where it should be, Mrs. Locke."

Her eyes skim over the rings on her finger.

"I'd say that I've never seen two people more in love, but that would be a lie." Lloyd chuckles. "Sela and I were just like you two once upon a time. If I can offer you any advice, I'd say to appreciate moments like this. Cherish every minute you're granted with each other."

"I do," I whisper as I stare into my wife's eyes.

"I do," she repeats before she brushes her lips against mine for a soft kiss.

"HAVE YOU CONSIDERED A CAREER IN MARKETING?" Hank Bartmess, the head of marketing at Abdons, asks Trina.

The question is rooted in sincerity because she just blew a hole in the proposed spring campaign.

Trina walked into this meeting prepared with flow charts, statistics, and a determined mind.

Lloyd, Hank, and I listened as she ripped apart the plan that's been in place for months.

Her approach is more targeted, cost-efficient, and social media based than anything we've done in the past.

The fact that she pulled all of that together today is impressive.

"I haven't." She tosses Hank a wide-mouthed smile. "Should I?"

Hank nods. "It's no secret that I'm retiring next year. We've got a good team in place, but no one like you."

That's because there isn't anyone on the face of this earth like her.

Scratching the side of her nose, Trina glances at me. "I like what I'm doing now, but no one can predict the future."

I want to.

I want to plan my future down to the minute when I'll draw my final breath.

Between now and then, I want to fill every second of it with time spent with her.

"I like this idea," Lloyd pipes up from where he's sitting across the boardroom table from me. "Graham and Trina are the company's dynamic duo."

That draws a hearty chuckle from Hank. "We all make a hell of a good team."

"We do," Trina echoes his thoughts. "Abdons has the best team in the business."

We do fine.

There are a few employees I'd fire today, but my current contract prohibits that.

Those people are still here because Lloyd is in their corner.

"I call this meeting adjourned." Lloyd laughs as he bangs his fist against the table. "It's time for a scotch."

Seeing as how we're nearing the end of the workday, I'm inclined to agree with him, but I have to opt-out.

"You don't have to ask me twice." Hank pushes back from the table. "Are you joining us, Mr. and Mrs. Locke?"

"I can't." I stand. "I have something to take care of."

That perks my wife's brows. "You do?"

Nodding, I reach out a hand as she glides to her feet. "I'll see you at home in a couple of hours."

"Where are you off to, Bull?" Lloyd asks as he rounds the table headed toward the door with Hank on his heel.

"I want to surprise my wife with something special."

Trina squeezes my hand, luring my gaze to her face. "You don't have to do that, Graham."

As tempted as I am to take her in my arms and kiss her, I resist that in favor of a soft brush of my lips against her cheek. "I do have to do it. I promise you'll like it, dear."

She catches my chin in her hand. Holding it there, she stares into my eyes. "I know I will, darling."

CHAPTER THIRTY-NINE

GRAHAM

I FIST my hand around the box containing the diamond earrings I just purchased for my wife.

I made a return visit to the same jewelry store I went to when I bought the engagement ring for Trina and my wedding band.

The woman who helped me that day was eager to lend a hand today. She set me up with a pair of earrings that will look beautiful on my wife.

I explained that they were a belated wedding gift, and after the store clerk sighed and commented on how lucky my wife is, she covered the box in wrapping paper and topped that with a glossy white ribbon.

Tucking the box into the inner pocket of my suit jacket, I swing open the door to a bakery.

I'm in Brooklyn at a place called Dobb's Bakery.

I've never been here before, but judging by the T-shirt Trina was wearing last night, she has been.

Normally, I'd stop by the bakery in the West Village that sells the over-baked cheesecakes that Lloyd thinks are the best thing in the world, but tonight I'm planning on putting a smile on my wife's face.

As soon as I step inside Dobb's, I'm greeted with the smell of vanilla and cinnamon.

I look around the eclectic space.

There are glass display cases filled with cakes, cookies, and dozens of other sugary concoctions.

A few tables sit in a corner surrounded by mismatched wooden chairs. The walls are lined with framed photographs. Some are of the bakery's interior, but many are of people.

I step closer to them to get a better look since there's a line of people five deep waiting to be served.

"Can you imagine having thirteen kids?" A deep voice comes at me from the left. "The Shaws are amazing people, aren't they?"

I glance over to see a man with graying temples. "The Shaws have thirteen kids?"

How the fuck did I not know that?

"And a few grandkids." He huffs out a laugh. "I've been coming here weekly for years. I know them all by name."

Without any urging on my part, he decides to prove that point. He starts rambling off names beginning with Elijah, then Gary, and Shirley. I can't keep up, but still, I listen intently until he says it. He says the name I've been waiting to hear, "and there's Trina and..."

Trina. Trina Shaw.

She's one of thirteen kids.

I turn back to the photo I had my eye on before this guy interrupted me. It's of a bunch of people, but the one who stood out to me when I first glanced at it is the same person I get to go home to tonight.

Trina, my wife and the woman I'm falling hard and fast for is front and center in a picture surrounded by people who resemble her. They all have smiles on their faces as they gaze at whoever was behind the camera.

It looks like the picture was taken in front of this place, judging by the red brick in the background.

"Every one of them took a turn working in the kitchen and behind the counter," he goes on, oblivious to the fact that I'm focused solely on my wife's image in the picture. "It must have been a hell of an experience growing up in this place surrounded by all that love. Herbert and Hermina Shaw are saints. They raised a group of amazing people and built up this bakery to what it is today."

Normally, envy would charge through me when hearing about someone's idyllic childhood and caring parents, but this time I'm grateful.

I'm grateful that Trina grew up in a home with people who loved her.

"Do yourself a favor and get a slice of the chocolate cake." The guy standing next to me laughs. "You'll be glad you did."

I turn to face him again. "Thanks for the tip."

My gaze trails to a woman standing behind the counter. I spot her resemblance to my wife right away. That has to be her sister.

I wandered in here looking for a dessert to surprise my wife with. I'm going to leave here with the knowledge that she's part of a loving family.

Our pasts couldn't be more different.

"YOU WENT TO DOBB'S?" Trina's voice cracks as she looks down at the pastry box on the kitchen island.

"I did."

I don't add anything, and she doesn't respond, so I reach for her hand.

I wrap it in mine and draw it up to my chest. Holding it there, I lower my voice. "I saw pictures of you on the walls. You have a big family."

Her blue eyes sear into me. "Did you meet anyone?"

"I saw Clara," I say the name of the woman behind the counter.

When my turn came to order, she was chatting with a man who wanted to order a birthday cake, so a younger guy stepped up to help me. He wasn't wearing a nametag and explained that he was a new hire. He dove deeper into that by sharing that he's a senior in high school, and his mom has been a regular customer at the bakery for years.

Since he wasn't related to my wife I didn't stand around making small talk with him after I ordered an array of sugary treats to bring home to her, even though she likely sampled them all at some point in the past.

"My sister," she whispers. "You didn't tell her that I'm your wife, did you?"

If I didn't care for her as much as I do, I might be pissed that she's so deeply concerned about her family catching wind of our marriage, but I doubt that she's told a soul outside the people we work with.

"She was busy with someone else, so a red-headed kid with freckles helped me."

That brings a small smile to her lips. "He must be new. Did he do a good job? Was he friendly and polite?"

I huff out a laugh. "He was nervous as hell, but he got the order right. I see no need for him to be fired yet."

"Clara never fires anyone." She chuckles. "Her heart is too soft for that."

I glance around to make sure Lloyd isn't lurking around the corner, peering into the kitchen at us. When I'm confident the coast is clear, I place my hand on Trina's chest between her breasts. "You have a soft heart too."

She glances down. "Are you trying to cop a feel right now?"

I inch my hand to the left to cup her tit in my palm. I squeeze it through the silk of her blouse. "I am now."

She drops her hand to grip my cock through my pants. It feels possessive in a way that makes me harden even more.

She leans forward to brush her lips against my neck. "I'll race you to the bedroom for a quickie before dinner."

Before she can say another word, I haul her over my shoulder and slap her round ass. "Quickies don't exist in this marriage. Dinner can wait. I'm taking all the time I need."

CHAPTER FORTY

Trina

GRAHAM TOUCHES his forehead to mine as he slowly undresses me. "You're a wonder to me, Mrs. Locke."

I don't correct him.

There are moments, this one included when I want to be Mrs. Locke. I want to have the name, the bond, and a future with him that will last for eternity, but we have an agreement.

There is an end date to all of this.

The fake marriage, the very real sex, and the feelings that have been blossoming inside of me since we exchanged vows have an expiry date.

I let my arms fall to my side after he's stripped me of my blouse and bra. "How so?"

His hands move behind me to draw the zipper of my skirt down. "There's so little that I know about you."

I smile at that. "It works both ways. I don't know anything about you."

My skirt is on the floor now, a red puddle of fabric at my feet. I move to kick off my heels as he drops to his knees.

He skims his lips over the silk of my panties, stopping to breathe in. "Here's a secret about me. I love the way you smell. I crave your taste."

My eyelids flutter shut as he pulls the fabric of the panties to the side to slide his tongue over my slick folds.

"IT HURTS TO MOVE." I cup a hand over my sex. "You were rough."

Graham glances at me as he tugs on the bottom hem of the T-shirt he just put on. "You're not complaining."

He's right. I'm not.

After he ate me to orgasm, I fell onto the bed while he sheathed his cock. Then, I climbed on top of him, straddling him as I rode him through another orgasm.

He told me then that it was his turn.

That's when he pushed me onto my stomach, grabbed my hips, and fucked me harder than he ever had before.

I buried my screams in the bed coverings as he grunted my name out again and again.

It was everything I wanted in that moment and more.

"I have something for you," he says as he stalks toward me.

I slip my panties on. "If it's your cock I appreciate it. I do, but my pussy needs a break."

That stops him mid-step. His head roars back in laughter.

It's a beautiful sight. The sound is joyful.

It makes me realize that I've rarely heard it.

"It's not funny," I fake protest. "You were so deep."

"Again, you're not complaining," he states as he stops in front of me.

I drop my hands to my hips, not caring that I'm only wearing a pair of panties and he's fully dressed. "I like it."

"I know." He brushes his lips over mine. "Close your eyes and give me your hand."

I do without a second thought.

My breath hitches when I feel the weight of something in my palm. "Can I look, please?"

Before he agrees, he kisses me again. This time it's demanding and meant to steal my breath.

"Wow," I whisper when he pulls back. "That was a gift in itself."

He laughs, his breath trailing over my neck. "Open your eyes, Mrs. Locke."

I take a second to savor the sound of that. When my eyes pop open, I glance down to find something wrapped in silver paper bound with a white ribbon. "What is it?"

"A belated wedding gift," he says. "See for yourself."

I hurriedly rip the wrapping paper free, tossing it on the floor. I steal a glance at my husband before I open the lid of a small white box. Inside is a pair of stunning earrings. There is no doubt in my mind that these are real diamonds. They are princess cut and have to be at least a carat each.

I gaze at Graham's face. "This is too generous."

His eyes search mine. "It's not nearly enough, Trina. It's a small token of my…"

I step in when his voice trails. I want to fill in the blank with the word love, but that's far-fetched. Graham doesn't love me. He appreciates me for helping him to make Mr. Abdon's dying wish a reality.

"Appreciation," I whisper.

He nods. "Right. It's a small token of my appreciation."

"I'll wear them tonight." I set to work removing the simple small gold hoops that I put in my ears this morning.

Graham reaches to tuck a strand of hair behind my ear. "The earrings will be all you wear when we fall back into bed later."

I fasten the clasp on one of the diamond earrings before I tug the other from the box. "Is that an order or a request?"

He laughs as he watches my every move. "It's your choice."

I adjust the earrings before I push up my chin. "How do they look?"

"They pale in comparison to your beauty," he says in a low tone. "But, I have to admit, they're perfect."

I move forward to kiss him softly on the corner of the mouth. "Thank you again, Graham."

"You're welcome." He reaches up to cup his hand over my cheek. "You need to get dressed. I'll order something in tonight. Then we'll feast on what I picked up at your family's bakery."

It'll be a taste of nostalgia in the midst of my complicated fake married life.

"You can tell me more about your siblings while you eat cookies, tarts, and cake." He pulls back. "I'll find Lloyd. You finish getting dressed."

"Graham." I grab his hand to stop him as he moves to leave the room. "Will you tell me about your siblings too? I don't know anything about your family."

I feel his hand tense in mine. "There's nothing to tell. I don't have any siblings. I don't have a family. I never have."

With that, he pulls away and leaves without another word.

CHAPTER FORTY-ONE

GRAHAM

THIS MARRIAGE WILL BE a part of me forever. The scent of my wife's skin, the vibrancy of her eyes when she stares into mine, and her touch – the way she touches me – will never leave me.

If all I get with her is the promised three months, I will live the rest of my days coasting through on the memories of moments like this.

I'll never want another woman the way I want Trina.

She sighs as she takes another small bite of the lemon tart that we're sharing.

I watch her carefully, taking note of the way her tongue slicks her bottom lip and the soft smile that settles on her mouth as she swallows the sweet treat.

"This cake is out of this world," Lloyd says from next to me as he devours the single slice of chocolate cake I bought.

He was in the library when I went to seek him out.

Neither of us mentioned that it was nearing nine by then.

I'd spent hours in bed with my wife as an appetizer to what I plan to do to her later.

I'm going to plant kisses over every inch of her body before I take her slowly.

I want the fuck tonight to last until daybreak.

Sleep is becoming a nuisance. It's time lost with Trina. Time I'll never be able to recover once she files for divorce.

"It's my mom's recipe," Trina states proudly. "She once told me it took her years to perfect it."

"It was worth it." Lloyd chuckles. "It's by far the best I've tasted in my entire life."

His entire life.

Those words draw Trina's gaze to mine. I see the sorrow that has settled in her eyes. I know what she's thinking. His life is nearing its end.

I want to change that, but I can't fix what ails Lloyd. I wish to hell I could.

"Graham bought samples of lots of different treats. I'll put the rest in the fridge for us to taste test tomorrow." Trina tries to lighten the mood. "Does anyone want coffee or tea?"

Lloyd shakes off the suggestion with a wave of his hand in the air. "Nothing for me. I'm going to find a book and get ready for bed."

I push back to lend him a hand as he stands. "I'll go with you to the library."

Trina stands too. "I'll put the dishes in the sink."

The T-shirt she's wearing inches up to reveal a sliver of the smooth skin of her stomach above the waistband of her jeans.

That's going to be the starting point for my kiss-fueled journey of her body tonight.

"You can load the dishwasher later, can't you, darling?"

I fight off a smile. "You bet, dear."

Trina bats her long lashes at me. "I'll clear the table and then take a bath."

I want in on that bath, so I place a hand on Lloyd's back to move him along.

He turns to face Trina. "Have I thanked you today for making Bull the happiest man alive?"

His words catch my breath in my throat because they're the truth.

"He makes me happy too," Trina responds. "He's a pretty great husband."

I glance at her. "I'll find you in a bit."

"You will." She wiggles both brows before her attention shifts to Lloyd. "Goodnight. Sleep well and dream good dreams."

"You too." He moves to kiss her cheek. "I'll see you in the morning."

I pray he does.

I want him to live forever, and it's not only because life will be hard without him.

When he's gone, this marriage is over, and I'm not ready for that.

I doubt like hell I ever will be.

"YOU GAVE her those earrings today, didn't you?" Lloyd asks as soon as we round the corner and enter the library.

I let out a light chuckle. "How did you know?"

His hand darts to his ear. "Trina kept touching them. She was checking to see if they were still there. That's a sure sign that a woman has just received new jewelry."

Shaking my head, I follow him into the room. "That's a hell of a lot more insight into women than I'll ever have."

He turns to face me. "You're learning, Bull. It's one step at a time."

I scan the shelves of books before my gaze settles back on him. "How are you feeling, Lloyd?"

"Good." He nods before he repeats the word with more exuberance. "Good."

"Have you given any more thought to my offer?"

He glances in my direction. "What offer?"

Seeing as how there is only one offer on the table, I remind him. "The offer to see another doctor. I'm going to do some research into who is the best cardiologist in the state. I'll convince them to make time for you."

"No need." He turns back to scan a row of books.

"I see a need," I press. "It can't hurt to get a second opinion."

"Reach that one up there for me." Lloyd points a finger to a shelf just out of his reach. "The book with the dark blue spine."

Frustrated that he's ignoring my suggestion, I take a few steps until I'm next to him. I slide the thick book free, taking note of the title.

A Fool's Grace.

Judging by the moody, dark cover image, I doubt this classifies as light-hearted reading.

I hand it off to him.

"I've read it twice," he confesses. "The charm in the prose is unrivaled. I get swept into the story every damn time even though I know how it ends."

I drop my gaze from his face to the book. "Maybe I should consider giving it a read when you're done."

His face beams with a wide-mouth smile. "You should, Bull. You should take advantage of all of this."

He arcs his hand in the air, and I follow its path with my

eyes.

I almost huff out a laugh when I catch sight of something odd perched on a shelf near the corner.

"This room is full of treasures," he goes on. "Reading can sweep you into another world. One where everything is exactly as you want it to be."

I'm feeling that now and it has nothing to do with any of the thousands of books lining the shelves.

I stalk toward the shelf holding the item I can't take my eyes off of. I point at it. "How long has this been here?"

Lloyd approaches me. "For as long as I can remember. It was here the day you moved in when you gave me a grand tour of the place."

Well, fuck.

Grinning from ear-to-ear, I shake my head.

"I'm heading to my room now." I feel Lloyd's hand land on my shoulder. "Tell your wife I adore her. You're a lucky man, Graham. Don't forget it."

"I won't ever forget it," I say because he's right. I may just be the goddamn luckiest man on this planet.

CHAPTER FORTY-TWO

Trina

I BARK out a laugh as soon as I exit the bathroom wearing only a white tank top and a pair of pink lace panties.

While I was busy getting out of the bath, Graham decided to strip and set himself in the middle of the bed. He's flat on his back.

That's not what has brought on my non-stop laughter.

It's the thing that's sitting atop his bare chest. He must have seen it in the library when he was in there with Lloyd.

"Trina." My name snaps off his lips with a groan. "You went for a drink with me that night because you wanted to."

I'm busted, and I don't even care.

"I told you that you had a pelican statue." I motion to where the ceramic statue is perched on his chest. "How could you not know that you owned that work of art?"

He reaches down to circle his hard cock with his hand. "I'm the only one who has ever referred to this as a work of art. I'm happy to know you see it the same way I do."

Still laughing, I sit my ass on the bed next to him. "I almost went to the library to get that pelican so I could win the bet, but a martini sounded too good to pass up."

Keeping his eyes pinned on my face, he gives his cock a slow stroke. "You didn't do it just for the drink. You wanted to go to that bar with me."

"Maybe," I say softly.

"You liked me even then."

"Don't push your luck." I move to grab the statue before I place it carefully on the nightstand next to the bed.

It can't be more than eight or nine inches tall, but it's charming in an abstract way.

Once it's set down, I crawl back onto the bed and onto my husband. I straddle him, settling so I can feel his cock pressing against my core.

He grips my thighs with his hands. "You like it, don't you?"

"Your work of art?" I perch a brow. "Or that pelican?"

"Both," he snaps the word from his tongue with a smile.

"The statue reminds me of one I saw a long time ago."

"When?" he asks instantly as his thumbs circle my inner thighs.

I rest a hand in the center of his chest to feel the steady beat of his heart. "I was eight."

His eyes travel over my face. "Eight-year-old Trina must have been an amazing kid."

Reaching for the bottom hem of my top, I tug it over my head to reveal my breasts. "I was a typical eight-year-old who had never been outside of New York City."

He watches me intently as I toss my top on the bed next to us.

"One of the regular customers at the bakery offered my parents their beach house on Long Island for a weekend."

"Complete with pelican statue?" Graham's hands move closer to my panties.

"One almost identical to that one was in the living room." I smile at the memory of the trip. "We only stayed a few hours. My folks couldn't leave the bakery for an entire weekend, so we made a late Sunday afternoon trip there."

Graham studies my face. "Those few hours meant the world to you, didn't they?"

"They meant everything," I whisper to control my emotions. "We ran in the sand and ate hot dogs we cooked over an open fire. We dipped our toes in the water. It was the best trip of my life."

"Because you were all together?" His voice has a tremor in it I've never heard before.

"Because we were all together," I repeat as I lean forward to brush his lips over mine.

He kisses me deeply, his tongue parting my lips softly. That draws a low moan from somewhere inside of me.

"Make love to me tonight," I say against his mouth as soon as the kiss breaks. "I want you to make love to me."

With effortless ease, he flips me over until I'm on my back, and he's staring down at me.

His hand moves to grip the side of my panties. "I'm going to ruin these, dear."

"Why am I not surprised, darling?" I ask with a smile.

"I'll buy you a few dozen new pairs," he promises with a soft kiss on my forehead.

I cup his face in my hands so I can gaze into his eyes. "Let me take the pelican statue with me when I move back home, and we'll call it even."

His brow furrows, but not a word escapes him. With a heavy exhale, he buries his face in my neck before he rips my panties from my body.

CHAPTER FORTY-THREE

GRAHAM

"YOU SHOW up empty-handed and expect me to let you in?" Kavan stands in the doorway of his home.

He's a penthouse dweller as well, but his is on Fifth Avenue in a building that has always been, and will always be, well out of my price range.

"I need to talk to you." I push past him, which isn't an easy task.

Kavan has a couple of inches on me and at least twenty pounds. He's in the best shape of his life. I am too, but still I wouldn't challenge him to a fistfight.

"C'mon in," he says with a sarcastic bite in his tone. "It's late. What the hell are you doing here?"

"I need a drink," I blurt out. "Something strong and…"

"Expensive?" he asks as he rounds me to head straight for a bar cart that sits near a bank of windows. "I'm giving you the cheap stuff since you showed up without warning. What if I had company?"

It's a rhetorical question.

Kavan doesn't invite people into his home or his world.

There are three people he tolerates. I'm one, and there's Sean and Harrison. Beyond that, his world consists of business associates and lawyers. He does his best to interact with all of them as infrequently as possible.

He pours me two fingers of Macallan 15.

I greedily take it and down it all in one gulp.

"Well, then." His arms cross his bare chest.

It's obvious I got him out of bed with my incessant knocking on his door. I bribed the doorman to let me up. It took five hundred dollars, but it was worth it because Kavan had ignored the three calls I made on my way over here. As soon as Trina fell asleep, I got up, put my clothes back on, and left.

Panic drove me over here.

"What do you want, Graham?"

"It's Trina," I say and then stop.

How the fuck am I going to explain what's going on to Bane when I can't make sense of it myself?

"You fucked her," he deduces the way he always does.

Nodding, I head toward the bar cart for a refill. "More than once."

I have no goddamn idea why I add that on. It hardly matters how many times I've taken my wife. I was lost to her the moment she agreed to marry me. My heart became hers when we kissed.

Now, she owns me through and through.

"Help yourself," Bane says as I fill my glass halfway.

I take another mouthful and savor it this time. The burn on my throat is exactly what I need.

"You're in love with her," he states as he walks toward me. "You've fallen in love with your fake wife."

I finish the drink before I turn to face him. "I don't know. I'm feeling things."

"Things?" His hands drop to his hips. He tugs on the waistband of the black pajama pants he's wearing. "That's vague. Is she feeling *things* for you too?"

I shake my head. "I have no fucking idea."

"Wrong answer."

"What the fuck does that mean?" I spit out the words at him.

He points a finger at me. "Your feelings scared the hell out of you, so you ran over here to hear me tell you to go back home and confess what you're feeling to your wife."

"I can't tell her," I argue. "If I do that, I'll have to tell her about my past. I can't start a real relationship with her until I tell her everything."

His chin lifts, his jaw tensing. "Your sins amount to nothing, Locke. Nothing."

He won't admit it, but I know that in his mind, he's comparing his sins to mine. He always does when I jump into a discussion about my past. Kavan often reminds me that I walked away from the person I used to be unscathed.

"Tell her what you did. You'll see forgiveness there," he says matter-of-factly.

"You don't know that," I bite back.

He steps closer to me. His eyes bore into mine. "I know that you think you did unforgivable things, but you didn't. You were a messed up kid doing screwed-up shit. Forgive yourself already. It's time."

I want to toss those words back at him, but I won't.

Kavan's past will trail him until the day he dies.

He'll never allow another person to get close to him. Any woman who enters his life is barred from it in a few hours.

He fucks for release. That's who he has become. It's how he'll remain.

"Go home, Graham." He gestures to the door.

"What if she feels nothing for me?"

He taps me on the side of my head. "You're an idiot. Do you think she screwed you because you're that goddamn irresistible? There are a lot of men in this city. She didn't jump into bed with any of them. Your wife chose you."

He's right. She did choose me. She wanted me as desperately as I wanted her, but it's a leap to go from wanting a fuck to falling in love.

"She might laugh in my face if I confess what I'm feeling."

He looks me over. "She might, but you won't know until you talk to her."

"This advice you're dishing out is surprisingly decent," I say as I pour myself another drink.

Kavan snatches the bottle from my hand and grabs a glass of his own. "It's common sense. That's something you've always lacked."

I wait until he's finished pouring his drink before I raise mine in the air. "Fuck you, Bane."

He ignores the gesture and instead swallows what's in his glass. "And a big fuck you to you. Now, finish that drink and get the hell out of here."

CHAPTER FORTY-FOUR

Trina

"WHAT'S on your schedule for today?" Graham asks from where he's standing near the door to the washroom.

He's freshly showered with a towel wrapped around his waist.

I could stare at him like this for hours, but I need to be somewhere soon even though I want to stay in this room with him all day.

I've been asleep the past two nights when he's gotten home from work. His days have been extra long since he's been immersed in negotiations with a new manufacturer.

Our mornings have consisted of a kiss between waking up and getting ready for the day.

Today, I made a point of getting up early to have a few extra moments with Graham before we both have to leave.

"I have a date in an hour," I toss that out so that I can see his reaction.

His arms cross his chest. "A date?"

Nodding, I adjust the front of the dark blue blouse I'm wearing. "A hot date."

He drops the towel to the floor, sending my jaw with it.

I stare because my husband is gorgeous. Every naked inch of him is a treat for the eyes.

He takes a step toward me. "I could fire you if you're late for work, Trina."

I tug on the zipper of my white skirt. "You won't."

A smile slides over his lips. "I may consider overlooking your tardiness if you tell me who the date is with."

"If I blow you, will you drop it?"

His deep laughter fills our bedroom. "You're going to blow me before you go on a date?"

I glance down at my watch. "I have time."

"On your knees," he orders as he nears me.

I reach out for his hand so he can help me lower myself to the floor.

As soon as I'm down, he fists his hard cock and trails the crown over my bottom lip. His eyes lock on mine. "Take it, Trina. Take it deep."

I close my eyes and slide my tongue over the plush head as I hear him hiss out my name.

THIRTY MINUTES LATER, I watch Graham put on a pair of gray pants. His skin is flushed, but he looks satisfied.

He should be.

He came with force. I swallowed every drop of his release before I stood and planted a kiss on his lips.

"What's your hot date's name?"

Laughter bubbles out of me. "I thought if I sucked your cock that I wouldn't have to divulge the details of my date."

Sliding on a white button-down shirt, he flashes me a smile. "I never agreed to that."

I stomp my foot on the floor. "You were too eager to get off."

"Your mouth does things to me, Trina." He straightens as he makes quick work of the buttons on the shirt. "I'm going to return the favor after our date tonight."

"We have a date tonight?" I ask with surprise edging my tone. "Did I miss the electronic invite?"

He disappears into the adjoining bedroom but returns seconds later with a dark blue tie in his hand. "I'm inviting you to have dinner with me tonight. There's a French restaurant called Sérénité that I think you'll like. They have a private dining room."

"A private dining room?" I repeat back. "That's fancy as fuck."

Shaking his head, he laughs. "It's perfect for what I have in mind."

I move toward him, taking the tie in my hands. "What do you have in mind? Sex in a restaurant? I've never indulged, but I could be persuaded."

He watches intently as I take control of the tie and slide it around his neck under the collar of his shirt. "I want to talk, Trina."

Suddenly, my hands start shaking. I busy them by knotting the tie.

"Do you want to talk about the new manufacturing facility?" I tilt my head. "I'm glad you finally hammered out a deal last night."

"Early this morning," he gently corrects me. "I didn't get in bed with you until almost three a.m., but that's not what I want to talk to you about."

"What is it then?"

His hands jump up to stall mine as I fumble with the tie. He holds them close to his chest. "Us. I want to talk about us."

My gaze trails from our joined hands to his face.

I look into his blue eyes. "Just us? Lloyd won't be there?"

He leans forward to brush his lips softly over mine. "I want my wife all to myself tonight."

"You'll have me all to yourself."

A smile tugs on the corners of his mouth. "Now, tell me about this hot date you have before work."

I finish with his tie, adjusting it until it's perfectly centered. "I'm having a cup of hot coffee with the best barista in the city. She's my neighbor and a friend."

His smile widens. "Take your time. My assistant has me out of the office for most of the day again. She works me to the bone."

I tug on his tie to bring his face closer to mine. "Your assistant knows what you're capable of. She knows how important work is to you."

His hand moves to my face. With the pad of his thumb, he traces my bottom lip. "It used to be the most important thing to me. It's not anymore."

Hope blooms inside of me that I'm the most important thing to him now. I want to be. He's quickly becoming the most important person in my life.

CHAPTER FORTY-FIVE

TRINA

AURORA SETTLES herself on the chair across from me.

It's been a hectic morning at the café, so her break was pushed back twice.

I used the time to respond to several work emails.

I may not be at the office right now, but that doesn't mean I can't keep on top of my work.

As I place my phone on the table, my gaze wanders to my bare hand.

I hid the rings in the compartment inside of my purse just before I walked in here.

My hand looks empty, and in some abstract way, I feel that way, too, knowing that I'm not wearing the rings Graham slid onto my finger.

"I'm sorry you've been waiting so long," Aurora says quietly. "It feels like half of Manhattan showed up here today for coffee."

I pick up my almost empty cup. "How can you blame them? You make the best in the city."

"It tasted fine to you?"

I laugh that off. "Fine? I wasn't joking, Aurora. It's fantastic coffee."

She tugs on the end of her ponytail. "I had a sip when I first got here, but that was all I could manage. It sent my stomach into a frenzy."

I lean forward to rest my elbow on the table. "How are you feeling now?"

"Better," she admits. "I am tired, though. That has nothing to do with the coffee and everything to do with my boyfriend."

I wiggle both brows. "Do I want details about that?"

"They would make you blush." She pats one of her cheeks. "I can't keep my hands off of Eldon lately."

"Lately?" I ask in a teasing tone. "I thought that was an ongoing thing."

"Fine." Both of her hands pop up in mock surrender. "I admit I can't get enough of him. That's a good thing, right?"

"It's the best thing," I say.

It's true.

I can barely keep my hands off of my husband. This morning was proof of that.

"Eldon told me that he has a major surprise planned for my birthday." She narrows her eyes. "Would you happen to know what that is?"

I laugh. "Is that why you asked me to meet you here? You want me to tell you what your birthday gift is?"

A broad smile coasts over her lips. "Yep."

I mime locking my lips shut and tossing the key over my shoulder.

"I'm going to take that as confirmation that you know

what it is." Her voice drops slightly. "Give me a hint, Trina. All I need is a tiny hint about what he got me."

Shaking my head, I sip the last bit of coffee from my cup.

"Did you promise you'd keep it a secret?" she asks.

I nod.

"Are you good at keeping secrets?" The corners of her lips edge up toward a grin.

"I am."

It's an understatement.

I've kept the fact that I'm married a secret. Now, I'm also holding tight to the knowledge that I've fallen in love with my husband.

"Could I persuade you to spill the beans with another cup of coffee?" She giggles. "This one would be on the house. I'll make it a large. I'll even throw in a bagel with extra cream cheese."

I reach over to squeeze her hand in mine. "I have to get to work. You're going to need to wait until your birthday to see what Eldon got you."

Her nose scrunches. "I'm horrible at being patient. In a perfect world, he'd surprise me early."

I push back to stand. "This imperfect world that we all live in has perfect moments. Your birthday is going to be one of them. I promise it will be worth the wait."

She studies my face. "I want you to have some perfect moments too. One day you'll find a man you love as much as I love Eldon. I know you will."

I have.

I found him, married him, and tonight could be the night he tells me he loves me too.

CHAPTER FORTY-SIX

Graham

I SET the box containing the custom-made watch on the table in front of the man I'm having lunch with.

Then, I take a seat across from him.

"This is it?" Crew Benton asks. "When you called to take me to lunch, I admit I was worried that you were trying to wine and dine me because you couldn't get the job done."

I push the box forward with my index finger. "Take a look."

He has the box open before I can take another breath.

"Fuck me, " he exclaims even though we're seated at a table in the middle of Nova with dozens of people within earshot. "This is a goddamn beautiful sight."

I huff out a laugh. "Is it everything you imagined it would be?"

That sends his gaze up to my face. "It's fucking amazing, Locke."

I can't mask my smile.

Hell, I'm grinning from ear-to-ear, and that's not just because he's happy with the one-of-a-kind watch.

I'm on cloud nine because I'm hours away from handing my heart over to the most incredible woman in this world.

"I'm glad you like it," I say as I glance around the restaurant for a server.

I'm saving the scotch for a meeting I have later this afternoon with one of the district managers at Abdons. I could go for a tall glass of water, though, and something to eat.

I traded breakfast for a blowjob.

I'd do it every day of the week, but it's left me hungry.

"Don't tell Harrison, but I like this one better than his." Crew chuckles.

He doesn't know the story of the watch on Harry's wrist. He barely knows Harry at all.

They met at a fundraiser early this year.

I was there too, because Harrison underwrote the entire thing. The cause was close to his heart, so he needed us all in his corner. Sean showed up in a tux, but as usual, Kavan bowed out.

It didn't matter.

We had a great time, and Crew Benton and his wife, Adley, made a contribution that rivaled the total of Sean and my combined donation that evening.

Crew is the Chief Operating Officer at Matiz Cosmetics. He works alongside his closest friend Nolan Black.

The watch that Crew can't take his eyes off of is for Nolan. He told me it's a gift to thank him for being a constant presence in his life.

I gave Harrison the first custom designed watch from Abdons last year.

He's worn it proudly every day since never hesitating to tell anyone who asks where he got it.

That has slowly opened a new door for Abdons. I'm still exploring the custom market, but the revenue we've generated so far is impressive, and every person who has ordered one has been more than pleased with their timepiece.

His gaze drifts from my face to my hand. "Wait a fucking minute, Locke. Are you married?"

I nod. "I am."

"That's a recent thing, isn't it?" He lifts his chin. "The last time we met up, you weren't wearing that ring."

"I didn't think you'd notice," I quip.

"Your watch is on your left wrist." He points out. "I was checking that out. I would have noticed the ring."

"It's fairly recent," I affirm with a nod.

"It's great, isn't it?" He shoves his left hand through his black hair. "Adley is the best thing that's ever happened to me. My kids are a close second."

I drop my gaze to my ring. "Trina is the best thing that's ever happened to me. "

"This calls for a wedding gift." He smiles. "What do you and Trina need? Or want?"

"We've got everything we could ever want," I say. "All that's left is for me to plan a honeymoon she won't soon forget."

"You haven't done the honeymoon thing yet?"

I shake my head. "When the time is right, I'll rent a house on the beach for a few days. She has fond memories of a place like that when she was a kid. I want to give her a new memory to add to that."

I want that for us. I want to marry my wife again and steal her away from this city to a secluded spot on a beach.

"Will a house in Westhampton Beach fit the bill? The

views are stellar and there's a private boardwalk with access to the beach."

I lean forward. "You know a place?"

He laughs. "I own a place. Consider it yours whenever you need it, Graham. I promise if you take her there, it'll be a honeymoon she'll never forget."

CHAPTER FORTY-SEVEN

Trina

LEAVING work early without permission is enough to send my boss's temper into overdrive, but I think today he'll make an exception.

I know he will.

I texted him twenty minutes ago to tell him that I had finished up everything I needed to get accomplished today. Then I told him that I plan to stop by my apartment to water my plant before I head to the penthouse to get ready for our dinner date.

His response made my heart sing.

Graham didn't text me back. He stepped out of the meeting he was in to call me.

He told me to bring the plant to the penthouse.

His exact words were, "Bring it home, dear."

I laughed even as tears of joy welled in the corners of my eyes.

It may just be a plant, but it's a symbol of the life that I had before I married Graham.

That life is about to change forever tonight.

I know that Graham didn't arrange this special dinner in a private dining room to drop some horrible news in my lap. He's going to confess what he's feeling, and I'm more than ready to hear it.

I want to do the same and tell him that I've fallen in love.

Taking quick steps on the sidewalk, I make my way to the lobby of my apartment building.

It pales in comparison to the building that I've called home for the past few weeks, but I've been comfortable here.

I made friends here that I know will last a lifetime.

Thinking of Aurora and Eldon reminds me to reach out to Asher.

I take a seat on a bench in the lobby and shoot my brother-in-law a quick text message.

Trina: **Hey! How are you?**

HIS RESPONSE IS QUICKER than I anticipated.

Asher: **Trina! I'm great. How about you?**

MY ANSWER IS honest and to the point.

Trina: **I've never been better. I have a favor to ask.**

MY PHONE RINGS ALMOST INSTANTLY.

I laugh because this is typical Asher Foster. If someone close to him requests anything, he'll make it a reality.

I answer immediately. "Hey, Asher."

"Trina," he says my name with what I know is a smile on his face. "What do you need?"

I sigh. "Your autograph."

That pulls a deep chuckle from him. "You want my autograph? Help me make sense of that."

I grin. "It's for a friend's birthday. Well, it's going to be the day she gets engaged too."

"This sounds special."

"It is." I nod, even though he can't see me. "Her boyfriend is going to propose on her birthday. He asked if I could get you to sign a card as an extra special treat."

"When's her birthday?"

"It's soon. On the twelfth," I respond quickly.

He's silent for a beat. "I can do one better. How about a private show? Maybe I can sing a song or two? I'll bring a guitar."

That sends me to my feet in excitement. "You're joking."

"I'm not." He laughs again. "What's your friend's name?"

"Aurora," I say with a huge smile on my face. "Her boyfriend is Eldon."

"I'm in." I hear the warmth in his tone. "You tell me where to be, what time to be there, and I'll do my best to give them a memory they'll never forget."

"You're the best," I say quietly. "You're the absolute best, Asher."

"Anything for my family, Trina. Falon is here. She sends her love. I'm sending mine too."

"I love you both." I gaze down at the floor. "I can't thank you enough."

"Falon wants to cook for you soon." He whispers something that I can't hear. "She says to bring a date when she does, or she's going to set you up."

I throw caution to the wind. "I'll bring a date. I'll bring someone special with me."

"I can't wait to meet him. Talk soon, Trina."

"Talk soon," I repeat before I end the call.

I STAND in my apartment and take it all in.

It may not be a large space, but it's been home to me.

All of the framed photographs on the wall of my family have made me feel as though I belong here.

I may not be taking those with me today, but I'll come back for them and everything else once Graham and I share what we're feeling.

A knock on the door turns me around.

It has to be Aurora. Since I haven't told my family about my marriage yet, I tug the rings off my finger and hide them behind the plant again. Aurora and Eldon both stop into the bakery sometimes, so I need to be careful at least until I can sit down with my parents and explain that I married my boss and then fell in love with him.

"I'm coming," I call out to her.

I make quick steps of the distance between where I'm standing and my apartment door.

I swing it open with a flourish, but instead of finding Aurora on the other side, I find my mom.

"Mom?"

"Trina," she whispers my name as her bottom lip quivers. "Sweetheart. I don't know what to say…I don't understand."

I step aside. "Mom, come in. Please."

Tugging on the bottom hem of the yellow blouse she's wearing, she steps over the threshold and into my apartment.

It was unusual to see my mom in anything but a plain white dress when I was growing up. It's what she wore when she worked in the bakery. She divided her time between the kitchen and the front counter.

Now that she's mostly retired, she wears vibrant colors. Today she's paired the blouse with a pair of white pants.

"Can I get you something?" I fumble my way through the question with a tremor in my voice. "Is everything okay?"

"I don't need anything." Her hand reaches out to find mine. "I went to your office, but they told me you left for the day."

"I left early," I admit. "What's wrong, Mom? Why didn't you call if you needed me? I would have come to Brooklyn."

"I know." She squeezes my hand. "I wanted to talk in person. In private."

I nod. "Talk about what?"

"A man came into the bakery today to get a chocolate cake. He said he had a piece the other night and loved it. He wanted an entire cake to take home with him."

My stomach knots as I ask the next question. "What man?"

"His name is Lloyd." Her blue eyes lock on mine. "Lloyd Abdon. He told me he owns the company you work for. He insisted that you and that man you work for are husband and wife. He said you married Mr. Locke."

The tears in her eyes cut through me. I see her confusion, her disappointment, and mostly I'm bearing witness to her pain.

"Is it true?" she asks in a whisper. "Did you marry your boss and not tell us?"

I choke back a sob. "It's true. I married him, Mom. I married my boss."

CHAPTER FORTY-EIGHT

Trina

I PLACE a mug of Earl Grey tea in front of my mom. I added a sprinkle of sugar just the way she likes.

She glances at me as I take a seat across from her at my small dining table.

My mom hasn't said a word since I admitted that I married Graham.

I know that she won't. She's waiting for me to explain all of this to her. I've spent the last five minutes gathering my thoughts while I prepared her tea.

"Lloyd is sick," I say.

She pushes a strand of her graying hair behind her ear. "He's sick?"

I nod. "He doesn't have a lot of time left."

Tears well in her eyes again. My mom's heart is the softest I've ever known. She rarely proclaimed her love with words when I was a child, but I'd always feel it around me.

She'd help us with our homework. She never missed a

parent-teacher conference or a school concert or play. Whenever one of us had a sporting event, she was front and center cheering us on. If we were sick, she nursed us back to health with homemade soup and hours spent giving up back rubs or putting cold compresses on our heads. She put her family first. Always.

"It's his heart," I go on, "Graham told me that Mr. Abdon wanted to see us married, so we decided to do it. We wanted to fulfill his dying wish. It was supposed to only be for a short time."

"Graham is your…" Her voice trails.

"My boss." I take a breath. "Graham is my husband."

Her gaze drops to my hand. "Lloyd told me he gave you his wife's ring."

I look at my bare hand. "He did."

"Can I see?"

Hesitantly, I get up from my chair and walk over to the potted plant. I grab the rings before I settle back down across from my mom.

"Why aren't you wearing them?"

The question isn't accusatory. I know she's confused. I don't think my mom has ever removed the plain silver band that my dad put on her finger on their wedding day.

It's a treasure to her. It's a symbol of the commitment she made to the man she's always loved.

"I wanted to tell you," I confess. "And dad. I wanted to tell everyone before I wore them all the time."

"You wanted to tell us you married a man you don't love?"

I slide both rings back on my finger before I look her in the eyes. "I love him, Mom."

That sends tears down her cheeks again. "You said you married him to fulfill Mr. Abdon's wish."

"We did, but things are different now." I hold back a sob. "We've spent a lot of time together. My heart knows he's the one, Mom. I love him."

"Does he love you?" I hear the plea in her voice.

I know that she only wants what is best for me. She wants me to be happy.

"I think he does," I say quietly. "We're supposed to talk about things tonight, but I feel it. I feel his love when he looks at me. I see it in his eyes. I hear it in his voice."

"He loves you." She smiles softly. "A woman knows when a man has given his heart to her."

My hands jump to the center of my chest. "I know."

She takes a sip of the tea and nods her head. That's her silent approval that it's exactly the way she likes.

I settle back into my chair and ask the question I've been dreading. "How is dad taking this?"

She sets the mug down carefully on the table. "I didn't tell him. I came here to talk to you first."

A sigh of relief escapes me. "Let me tell him, Mom."

"I think that's best." She nods. "I think you and your husband should tell him together."

I like that idea.

"We will."

She scrubs a hand over her face. "There's something else, Trina. I'm sorry for this, but…"

"What is it?" I interrupt her, suddenly feeling the knot reforming in my stomach.

Her eyes close briefly. "I didn't know what was happening. I had no idea what was going on, so when Mr. Abdon told me you were married, I told him he was wrong."

I listen intently, hoping that's as far as their discussion went.

She shakes her head. "I told him that there's no way any

daughter of mine would marry a man without telling her family."

Dread drops over me. "What did he say, Mom?"

"He didn't know what to say." She shrugs. "I told him that you weren't at all fond of your boss. I said that the last time I saw you that you didn't have any wedding rings on and you never mentioned a husband. I told him we had lunch at your apartment together that day."

I drop my gaze to my lap.

"He asked where we had lunch and I told him here." She sighs. "I said your apartment is on West Forty-Third Street, and I came here with sandwiches after I went to the library. He wanted to know what day that was. I told him. It seemed very important to him, Trina, so I told him."

I can't be angry with her. My mom is the most honest person I've ever known.

"I'm sorry," she apologizes. "He left the bakery in tears, Trina. He was very upset."

I reach across the table to take her hand in mine. "It's okay, Mom. It's all going to be okay."

I say that even though I know nothing is okay. The lie that Graham and I concocted to make Mr. Abdon's dying wish a reality may actually break his already fragile heart.

CHAPTER FORTY-NINE

Trina

I CURSE under my breath as the call goes directly to Graham's voicemail again.

"Please, Graham, please." I try to calm my voice, but it's useless. "This is an emergency. You have to call me now."

That's the third time I've tried to call him in the past five minutes.

The first time was when I said goodbye to my mom on the sidewalk outside of my building.

I got her into a taxi that I flagged down and then pressed the button on my phone to connect me with Graham.

Tears fell as I left him a voicemail message.

Then I checked his calendar on my phone. He's in a meeting with one of the district managers for Abdons.

He told me that he was going to meet up with him for a drink, but he didn't say where.

Dammit, I wish I knew which bar he was in.

Frustrated but determined to handle this catastrophe, I edge forward on the backseat of the Uber I'm in.

"We're almost there." The woman behind the wheel smiles at my reflection in the rearview mirror. "You seem anxious to get to where we're going."

"You have no idea," I whisper.

"Maybe I do," she bounces back at me. "I can see you're a bundle of nerves. I'm all ears if you need to talk."

I manage a soft smile even though my world is currently crumbling around me. "I appreciate that. I really do, but I'm all right."

She nods. "Whatever it is, it's going to work out."

I wish I had her confidence.

I need to face Mr. Abdon alone.

Taking a deep breath, I close my eyes and make a silent wish that Graham will call me back before I step foot in the penthouse. I need him to help me find the right words to tell the most important man in his life why we've been lying to his face for weeks.

LLOYD IS WAITING in the foyer when the elevator doors slide open.

I can tell that he's been crying.

His eyes are red, his cheeks ruddy, and his shirtsleeves are rolled up to his elbows. I've rarely seen him without a suit jacket on.

"Trina." My name escapes him in a muted tone.

"Mr. Abdon," I say quietly, sure that I've lost the privilege of calling him Lloyd.

He approaches me with uneven steps, so I instinctively

reach out a hand to help steady him. Surprisingly, he takes it in his.

"You look the way I feel," he says, studying me. "I take it you spoke with your mother?"

"She came to see me," I admit.

"So it's true?" he asks with sorrow edging his tone. "Your mom had no idea you were married? You've been hiding that from your family?"

I nod. "They didn't know."

"Why not?" he spits the question out. "Why on earth would you keep that from them?"

I wish I had an easy answer that would spare him pain, but I don't. "It's hard to explain, sir."

"What about Graham?" he asks with a perked brow. "Can he offer me an explanation? He's ignoring my calls."

"He's not," I stress both words. "He's in a meeting, sir. It's an important meeting."

"I should have realized what Graham was up to." He drops his gaze to the floor. "A couple of weeks ago, Eugene mentioned what a breath of fresh air you are. He said he hadn't known you very long, but I didn't think to ask when he first met you."

I don't offer up those details, hoping he'll skip past them.

"Had you been in this building before the day you and Graham picked me up from the airport?"

As guilt grips me, I look him in the eye. "That was my first time. I'd never been here before then."

"I'm sorry that you got caught up in this." He exhales sharply. "I thought Graham had changed. All of these years, and I thought he'd stopped with the lying and the games. I was wrong. I was so wrong."

"Sir," I whisper. "Let me try and explain."

"You have nothing to explain," he cuts in before I can get another word in. "I know that Graham put you up to this. He must think this marriage will secure his position as the future owner of Abdons. I suppose it shouldn't surprise me. Why did I think he was a better man now than that kid I met so long ago?"

I want to ask about the day they met, but I can't. This isn't the time.

"It's not what you think." I stop to mentally form my next sentence. I want to word this correctly so that Mr. Abdon understands that we may have started out trying to make his wish a reality, but somewhere along the way, it became all too real.

I'm Graham's wife. I feel it in my bones.

"It's exactly as I think," he snaps, then shakes his head. "I'm sorry, Trina. I worked so hard to help Bull. I dropped the charges. I spoke to his foster parents. They were thrilled when I told them I wanted to send him to The Buchanan School so he could clean up his act. Frankly, they were relieved that he'd be in a boarding school. I paid for college. I even gave him a job working for me. Ironically, I was very close to signing the company over to him, but not now. I will never hand my life's work to him after this."

"What charges?" I question. "I don't understand."

"He still hasn't told you?" he asks before he chuckles sarcastically. "Of course, he hasn't. He never had any intention of telling you. This wasn't a real marriage at all, was it?"

That stings more than it should. He's right about the fact that I know nothing about Graham's past.

"Am I safe to assume that you don't know how we met?" He lifts his chin. "He didn't tell you about that either, did he?"

I shake my head.

"I kept pushing him to tell you, but why would he? You're not really his wife."

I fight back tears.

"Allow me to fill in the blanks for you." His arms cross his chest. "He broke into our flagship store when he was fifteen. The security company called me before they called the police. I lived nearby at the time, so I got to the store before they did."

I stare at him, stunned into silence.

"I walked in to find a messy-haired kid with a bull tattoo on his arm and twelve of my watches in his hands and his pockets."

My hand jumps to cover my mouth.

"He had been through ten foster homes by that point." He leans closer to me. "Ten. He kept doing things that would get him kicked out. He was fighting, stealing, causing trouble with anyone he could. Sela and I stepped up and helped him. We got him into the most exclusive private school in the state for boys. We saw him through to his college graduation."

"I didn't know."

"He had no one until we came along." He shakes his head. "Absolutely no one, and this is how he repays me. He pulls the wool over my eyes. He makes a nice young woman like you go along with his charade. He made a fool out of me."

"Sir, please." I take a step toward him.

"His mother left him on a subway train when he was six." He shakes his head. "I felt sorry for him. Sela did too. No father and his mother abandoned him. His grandmother wanted nothing to do with him. We thought we could help him get on the right path."

My heart aches in my chest for the boy Graham once was,

a boy who had no one to turn to. He had no family. No one to love him the way my parents have always loved me.

The only person who cared enough to help him is livid at the moment, and it's in my power to change that.

I can give this to Graham. I can help him salvage the family he does have.

"None of this was Graham's idea." I swallow past the lump in my throat. "I'm the one who suggested we get married, sir."

His brow furrows. "You?"

I take a breath to steady myself. "He let it slip that you haven't been well and that you thought we'd make a great couple, so I told Graham we should get married."

"Graham went along with this?" he asks skeptically. "You came up with the plan to tell me you two were dating and then engaged and married? Are you even legally wed to each other, or is that another lie?"

"We were married at the courthouse," I confess. "Graham told me that he couldn't lie to you about being married if we weren't. He said you were the best man he's ever known, sir."

I see the tension in his shoulders slip away as he contemplates everything I'm saying. "Is there a prenup? Did Graham consider that? I hope to hell he thought of that."

"I signed one," I say quickly. "Graham loves you, sir. He would never intentionally hurt you."

"What about you?" His finger flies in the air toward me. "What are you getting out of this? You must be benefiting in some way?"

This is it. This is where I sacrifice myself to save my husband. "I negotiated a one and a half million dollar payout in exchange for three months of marriage."

He rakes a hand through his hair. "I can't believe this."

I watch as his gaze falls to my left hand. I tug my

wedding rings off, suddenly feeling unworthy of both rings but especially guilty of wearing the ring he gave his late wife.

I shove both rings at him. "I'm so sorry, Mr. Abdon."

He takes the rings in his palm. "Bull went along with this to make me happy? He did that for me? It's not about the company?"

The tide has changed. I see it in the way he's looking at me. Graham will be spared his pain. It's a burden I can carry for the man I love.

"He did it for you," I whisper. "All he wanted was to make you happy."

"It might be best if Graham and I had some time alone when he comes home." He glances behind me at the elevator. "I'm sure you understand, Miss Shaw."

That cuts through me. I'm no longer Mrs. Locke in his eyes.

"I'll go home," I say because that's what my apartment is.

I don't belong here anymore.

"Goodbye, Trina." He doesn't make a move toward me.

"Goodbye, Mr. Abdon. I hope you know just how deeply Graham loves and admires you."

His response is a curt nod, so I turn, press the call button, and step onto the elevator that will take me back to the life I had before I married the man of my dreams.

CHAPTER FIFTY

GRAHAM

FEAR.

That's all I feel when I finally glance at my phone after my meeting.

I silenced it because Kay was on a texting spree. She's sure that the design she's currently working on is just as great as the one Lloyd chose for the spring campaign.

She's wrong.

Her latest creation is too big of a leap back in time.

I told her that when I replied to her first text message. She took it as a pun and kept pressing me to sign off on including this latest design in the spring launch too.

It's not going to happen.

I'll tell her as much when I have more time, but from the number of text messages and voicemails waiting for me, something isn't right.

I count three voicemails from Trina along with a few texts

asking me to call her right away. There are a couple of voicemails from Lloyd too, but the one text that sends fear coursing through me is from Eugene.

It's the last message to arrive, and it's ominous.

> *Eugene:* **Mr. Abdon was taken to Lennox Hill Hospital by ambulance. It's urgent! Urgent, sir!**

I TAKE off down the sidewalk in the direction of the hospital as I call Trina. It rings through to voicemail, but I disconnect before leaving a message. Instead, I call up the messages she left me.

I listen to one and then the other two.

I hear the panic in her voice as she pleads with me to call her.

Next, I listen to one of the voicemails Lloyd left me.

"Graham," he says my name followed by an unmistakable sob. "Where are you? I need you to come home."

"Fuck," I mutter before I try Trina's number again.

She doesn't answer.

She must be at the hospital with Lloyd.

It's too soon. It's too fucking soon for me to lose him.

I glance at the street to see an available cab. I dart onto the street, racing toward it. I dodge around a delivery truck. The guy behind the wheel blares the horn right before he tells me to wake the fuck up.

I wish to hell I was asleep and in the middle of a nightmare, but I'm not.

I hop into the cab and tell the driver to get me to Lennox Hill as fast as he can. I only hope I make it there in time.

"MR. ABDON COULDN'T CATCH his breath," Eugene explains. "I called an ambulance immediately."

"You did the right thing," I reassure him.

I was shocked to see him standing near the reception desk in the emergency department when I sprinted in here, but the man takes his job seriously. He must have felt the need to trail the ambulance in case he could help Trina in some way.

I ran right past Eugene in search of information about Lloyd, but the woman working the desk told me to sit tight.

How the fuck do you sit tight when you're facing the death of someone you love?

"He fell ill right after Mrs. Locke left."

My head snaps in Eugene's direction. "Left? She's not in the examination room with him?"

"No, sir." He shakes his head. "She ran out of the building in tears. Less than five minutes later I got the call from Mr. Abdon that he was feeling dizzy and having trouble breathing."

What the fuck is going on?

"Trina didn't say anything to you about what was wrong?" I press on, "Why was she crying?"

"I'm not sure." He shrugs. "She arrived home in a rideshare, I think. I called out to her, but she raced toward the elevator and boarded it quickly. Ten minutes later, she was back in the lobby in tears. Then she left and ran down the sidewalk before I could catch her."

"Excuse me?" A man's voice cuts into our conversation.

I turn to see a nurse next to me. "Yes? What is it? You have news?"

"The doctor is still examining Mr. Abdon, but we have his possessions." He shoves a small zip-top plastic bag toward Eugene. "You came in with him, right? I can leave these with you."

I snatch the bag from him. "I'm the closest thing he has to family."

The nurse nods. "As soon as Dr. Fuller is done his examination, he'll be out to speak with you."

Nodding, I swallow. "Thank you."

"Is there anything I can get you while we wait?" Eugene asks.

"You can go back to your post." I glance at him. "I can handle it from here."

"The incident with Mr. Abdon happened in the middle of a shift change. Roger is on duty now." He straightens the lapels of his jacket. "If it's all right with you, I'd like to stay, sir. No one should wait for news in a hospital alone."

I nod. "I appreciate that."

He pats my shoulder. "I'm going to give my wife a quick call to let her know where I am."

As he wanders off, I drop my gaze to the plastic bag in my hands.

The watch that is always on Lloyd's wrist is there, as is his wedding ring. His wallet takes up most of the space in the bag, but I do a double take when I turn it over.

At the bottom of the bag are two rings. One is the diamond engagement ring I gave my wife. The other is the wedding band I slid on her finger before I kissed her for the very first time.

Why did Lloyd have these?

With a shaking hand, I tug my phone out of my pocket and try Trina's number again.

As soon as it rings through to voicemail, I clear my throat. "Trina, call me."

I hang up, leaving it at that because what the fuck else am I going to say? I feel like I lost the only woman I've ever loved, and the man who saved my life is fighting for his. I don't know how the hell to change any of it.

CHAPTER FIFTY-ONE

Trina

I GLANCE down at my phone and the voicemail notification that has popped up on the screen.

It's from Graham.

It arrived more than two hours ago, but I haven't been able to bring myself to listen to it.

I can't.

After I got back to my apartment, I flung myself onto my bed and cried. I wept for the pain that I saw on Mr. Abdon's face. But, most of all, I sobbed because Graham has lived through so much.

There's no way I could have known that he grew up in such turmoil.

My heart breaks for the boy he was. At the same time, I'm proud of the man he's become.

I roll over and stare out into the darkness beyond my bedroom window.

I used to feel content here.

At one time, this apartment was a symbol of the life I wanted.

I craved the independence that living alone in Manhattan gave me. I celebrated the fact that I'd landed a job all on my own, and I welcomed the chance to get to know the men I'd date.

I don't want that life anymore.

I want the life that I had with Graham.

It's not the penthouse I desire or the diamond earrings. It's the moments when he'd look into my eyes or touch me. It was the sound of his laughter and the way he tried to make me as comfortable as he could there.

I felt at home in that vast penthouse because he was there.

A sob escapes me as I think about what I've lost.

I can't make him choose between Lloyd and me, and I know that there's no way Mr. Abdon will remain a part of Graham's life if I'm his wife.

I have to follow through with the divorce.

I rub a hand over my forehead.

I'll still be Trina Shaw when this is over, even though I now wish that I had changed my surname to Locke so I could have been Trina Locke even for a brief moment in time.

I move to sit up just as I hear a soft knock on my apartment door.

I want Graham to be on the other side of it. I want him to scoop me into his arms and tell me that we'll get through this together, but I doubt it's him.

He hasn't tried to call or text me other than the brief voicemail he left me hours ago.

I can't blame him for giving up. I didn't respond to him.

It breaks my heart to think that he must feel as though I've abandoned him just as so many people have.

The person at my door knocks harder.

I swing my legs over the side of the bed and push up until I'm standing.

Straightening the front of my blouse and skirt, I walk out of my bedroom, just as an even louder knock sounds through my apartment.

I swing open the door.

"Trina, help me. I'm sick," Aurora mutters before she stumbles forward and into my arms.

"I'M FEELING BETTER," Aurora whispers. "It's probably just food poisoning. I had take-out tonight. Maybe that's what it is."

I lead her through the sliding doors of the emergency department at Lennox Hill Hospital.

After she showed up at my apartment door and almost fainted, I sat her on my couch with a glass of water.

She felt nauseous as soon as she had a sip. As she ran to my bathroom, I ordered an Uber, and we headed out together.

My sister, Shirley, had food poisoning once and ended up in the hospital for three days. Being proactive can't hurt. If anything, a doctor can give Aurora something to calm her stomach enough that she can at least keep fluids in.

"I can call Eldon and your parents," I offer as we approach the reception desk. "Do you want me to do that?"

"My folks are driving home from a wedding in Indiana. They're sightseeing along the way. They won't be back for another two days." She glances at me. "Let's wait to call Eldon. His shift ends in a couple of hours. I don't want him to think he has to rush here because I have a stomach ache."

I offer her a smile. "We'll wait."

"If you need to be somewhere, I can wait alone."

The only place I need to be is in my bed crying my eyes out.

I squeeze her hand. "I'm not going anywhere."

"Thank you for this, Trina."

"Anything for you." I pull her into a side embrace. "I'm here for as long as you need me."

I mean it.

My life may be in tattered ruins right now, but I will stay in this hospital for as long as Aurora needs me to. Maybe by the time she's discharged, I will have figured out what my next step should be.

CHAPTER FIFTY-TWO

Graham

"I'M DR. MORGAN." The man standing in front of me extends a hand. "Gaines Morgan."

I take his hand in mine. "Graham Locke. It's good to meet you."

I glance past him to where Lloyd is resting. He's been transferred to the cardiac care unit. The doctor in the emergency department assured me that Lloyd would be in the hands of one of the best cardiologists in the city.

I assume I'm talking to him.

"Is this the end?" I blurt out. "He told me he doesn't have long to live. Will I get a few minutes with him to say goodbye?"

Dr. Morgan rubs a hand over his chin. "Lloyd told me the same thing. He's mistaken."

Shaking my head, I try and absorb what he just said. "I don't understand."

"I spoke with his cardiologist in Paris."

"You did?"

"Briefly." He chuckles. "I got him out of bed. He happens to be an old friend of a friend."

I rake a hand through my hair. "What did he tell you?"

He crosses his arms over his chest. "One of the arteries in Lloyd's heart has narrowed. To repair that, we need to insert a cardiac stent in the artery. That will open it and allow the blood to flow freely."

I move slightly to the left to get a better view of Lloyd. "He knew that before he left Paris?"

"He's known that for some time."

"Why was he waiting to have it done?" I try and make sense of it all. "It's a fairly straightforward procedure, isn't it? The mother of a friend of mine had it done a few years ago."

"It's very straightforward."

"What the hell?" I fist my hands at my sides. "I'm missing something here. He told me his heart wasn't going to last much longer. He made it sound as though he had only a few months to live."

Dr. Morgan's hand jumps to my shoulder. "Lloyd believes all of that. He didn't hear it from a doctor. His heart is telling him that."

I shake my head. "What?"

"Mr. Abdon has a broken heart." He lowers his voice. "I've seen this before. It's not uncommon after devastating losses."

I swallow to contain my emotion. "His wife's death…"

"Has been more than he can bear," he goes on, "Lloyd doesn't feel hopeful. He is in deep emotional pain, and to him, even this simple procedure seems unnecessary."

"He wants to die?"

He steps back. "It's not a conscious decision. He's given

up. He's experiencing a level of grief that is impossible for most people to grasp."

I silently curse myself for not seeing this. I didn't comprehend the depth of Lloyd's struggle after Sela's death.

"He was distraught before I sedated him," he goes on, "Lloyd wanted out of here so he could get to the scattering garden before sunset. I told him the sun had set hours ago, but he wanted me to call him a car to take him to New Jersey."

I stare at him. "He wanted to go to New Jersey?"

"To the memorial park," he says it as though I'm completely aware of what the hell he's talking about. "My grandfather is in that same scattering garden. It's a beautiful place, isn't it?"

After Sela's funeral, Lloyd explained that she wanted her ashes spread in a special spot. She also wanted to live out their last days in Paris. They never had time to make that a reality, which is why Lloyd was insistent on moving to France. He told me he wanted to make her wish come true. I assumed that's where he spread her ashes.

I take a stab in the dark. "Sela is there too."

He nods. "And LJ. I can't fathom the pain of losing a child. Lloyd spoke about his son with such reverence and grace. He sounds like he was an amazing young man."

"WHAT'S OUR NEXT STEP?" I ask Dr. Morgan when he comes back into Lloyd's room.

Another doctor called him out into the corridor, but he assured me with a pat on my back that he'd be back within ten minutes.

A glance at my watch tells me he's a man of his word. Only eight minutes have passed.

I've spent every second of those eight minutes at Lloyd's bedside watching him sleep, trying to make sense of the fact that he had a son. He has never once mentioned LJ to me.

"I want to get that stent in his heart," he says clearly. "I need his permission for that, so once the sedation wears off, I'll have another go at him. I'm a persuasive bastard. I'm confident we'll get it done today."

I let out a chuckle. "You seem like the man for the job."

He nods.

"I wasn't around when he was brought in." I blow out a breath. "The doorman…a friend, Eugene, was with him. I'm not clear on what was happening. Was Lloyd in pain? Was he having trouble breathing?"

He looks over to where Lloyd is still asleep. "I think the weight of his grief got the best of him today. His blood pressure spiked. His blood sugar was low. It was a combination of a few things."

"I see."

"Fate may have played a hand in it too."

"Fate?" I raise my chin. "How so?"

"After speaking with Lloyd, I got the sense he would have ignored his heart issues indefinitely. What happened today was his saving grace. I'm going to do everything in my power to get that stent in before he walks out of here. With some healthy diet habits and an exercise regime, I believe Lloyd has many good years left."

"You're serious?"

Dr. Morgan smiles. "Grief therapy can help him tremendously but let's take this one step at a time. I'll be back to work my charm once he wakes up."

I reach to shake his hand. "Thank you. I can't thank you enough."

"He has a good heart." He pats the center of his chest. "It

may need some work now, but fundamentally with some patience, love, and attention, Mr. Abdon can get through this. I'll do my part."

"And I'll do mine," I say because I will.

I'm going to help Lloyd find a path out of his grief, and I'm going to find my wife. I need her. I want her, and I have to figure out why the hell Lloyd had her wedding rings.

CHAPTER FIFTY-THREE

Trina

"HOW ARE YOU DOING?" Dr. Gavin Fuller walks into the exam room with a smile on his face.

We've been in the emergency department for almost two hours.

Dr. Fuller greeted Aurora as soon as we were brought to this room. He introduced himself and explained that he wanted to hook her up to intravenous fluids. He told us that his concern was that she was becoming dehydrated.

Since then, blood has been drawn, and a nurse came in to ask Aurora a variety of questions related to her medical history.

I tried to excuse myself, but Aurora insisted that I stay.

I was happy to.

Sitting next to her bed, telling her stories about my siblings and the bakery has kept her smiling.

"I'm tired," Aurora admits. "Can I go home?"

"Soon." He glances at me. "How about you? How are you?"

He's a handsome guy, and before I was married, I'd flirt shamelessly with him, but my heart belongs to only one man.

"I'm good." I shift my gaze to Aurora. "I'm concerned for Aurora. She almost fainted in my arms tonight."

I told the nurse that story earlier.

He typed something into the tablet in his hand and thanked me for the extra details.

I have no idea if he was being polite or if that bit of information was important.

Dr. Fuller looks at the tablet he's holding. "I have your blood tests results, Ms. Salik."

"It's Aurora," she insists. "Please call me that."

"Aurora," he repeats her name with a grin. "I want to double back to something before I share the results."

"I can step out." I point to the corridor outside the room. "I'll try calling Eldon again."

I've left two voicemail messages so far for Aurora's boyfriend. I was calm as I explained that we're at Lennox Hill Hospital because Aurora thinks she has food poisoning.

It wasn't an official diagnosis, but I didn't want to leave a message with fewer details than that because I don't want Eldon to panic.

"Please stay." Aurora reaches for my hand. "I'm sure it's just something I ate, but I'd like you here with me."

I nod. "I won't go anywhere."

Dr. Fuller rubs his chin. "You told the nurse that your last period was a few weeks ago. Is that right? Was it lighter than normal? Shorter?"

My heart beats faster.

I know exactly where this is headed.

How did I not see this at my apartment when Aurora ran off to the bathroom?

"I don't know how that relates to food poisoning." Aurora shrugs.

Dr. Fuller steals a glance at me. I see the smile on his face.

"Humor me, Aurora."

She barks out a laugh. "You're the doctor, so okay. I don't keep close track of my cycle, but I think it was three weeks ago. It might have been four, or…"

"More?" he interrupts.

She nods. "It could have been. Work is busy, and I haven't told anyone, but I'm going to apply to nursing school."

My hand leaps to my mouth. "Aurora, that's incredible."

"I don't have what it takes to be a doctor." She turns to Dr. Fuller. "I know I'll make a great nurse, though. I'm compassionate. I'm kind. The sight of blood doesn't make me squeamish."

The doctor tilts his head as a grin ghosts his mouth. "You're also pregnant."

Aurora's head snaps in my direction before she turns back to look at him. "Say again, please."

"You're pregnant, Aurora," he says softly. "Almost eight weeks pregnant. Congratulations."

Tears fill her eyes, falling onto her cheeks. "I'm going to be a mom and a nurse?"

I squeeze her hand. "I'm so happy for you."

"I'm happy for me," she says excitedly. "We weren't trying. We're careful. I'm on the pill."

"Without any other protection, there's always a slim chance of pregnancy when you're on oral birth control." Dr. Fuller types something into his tablet. "The nausea is part of the first trimester fun. It should pass as your pregnancy progresses."

"I need vitamins." Aurora taps her forehead. "One of my co-workers is pregnant, and she's taking special vitamins."

"We'll get that all sorted." Dr. Fuller pats her hand. "I'll be back shortly to talk about prenatal care and to get you set up with an obstetrician."

"Thank you, Doctor," she says as he turns to leave.

He glances over his shoulder. "I'm honored I could share this news with you, Aurora. I wish you and your husband nothing but the best. His name is Eldon, right? I heard you mention his name to your friend."

Boyfriend," Aurora corrects him. "Eldon is my boyfriend."

I'm about to blurt out that he'll soon be her fiancé, but I don't. I look down at my bare ring finger.

This morning I had a husband. Now, I have an ache in my chest that I've carried with me since I left the penthouse. Something tells me it will always be there.

I MAKE my way to the doors of the emergency department as soon as Eldon sends me a text telling me he's arrived.

He barges in as the sliding glass doors part for his arrival.

Wearing his police uniform and with a stoic expression on his face, he looks imposing.

I know he's scared.

In mere moments he'll be on cloud nine, knowing that the woman he adores and wants to marry is expecting their first child.

"Trina!" he calls my name as he rushes toward me. "Where's Aurora? How is she feeling?"

"She's in an exam room." I point in the direction of the corridor I just came from. "She's good, Eldon. She's going to be so happy to see you."

"I've been worried sick," he admits. "I could kick myself for not texting you when I saw your first message. I thought it was about her birthday and the card Asher was signing. I was busy. I assumed it could all wait."

"You're here now." I smile. "Go to her. I'm going to wait out here."

"What room is she in?"

I glance toward the corridor again, but something catches my eye. It's a person. A man with graying hair raises his hand in greeting.

"Trina?" Eldon questions. "Are you all right?"

"I see someone I know," I whisper. "I hope he's okay."

"I'll find Aurora," Eldon says before taking off toward the corridor. "You check on your friend."

As he sprints away, I stare at the man in the doorman's uniform who is approaching me.

"Eugene?"

"Mrs. Locke." He smiles. "You're here for Mr. Locke, aren't you?"

Panic darts through me as I scan the faces in the waiting room in search of my husband's. "Graham? Where is he? What's wrong?"

He shakes his head. "I'm sorry. No, no, it's not Mr. Locke. It's Mr. Abdon. They've admitted him to the cardiac care unit. Mr. Locke is with him now. I assumed you came to be with him. He's pretty shaken up."

"Is Lloyd all right?" I question as I swallow back a sob. "Is he going to be okay?"

"I'm not sure." He steps closer to me. "After you left

earlier, he wasn't feeling well. He had trouble catching his breath."

This is my fault. All of this is my fault. I upset Lloyd, and this is the result.

"Why don't you head up there?" He shoves two cups filled with coffee at me. "I ran down to the cafeteria to get these. I'm sure Mr. Locke would prefer to see your face instead of mine right now."

I'm not as sure as he is, but I push everything that happened earlier aside. I have to face this and my husband. If by chance, I'm granted a moment with Mr. Abdon before he passes, I need to apologize to him again and thank him for giving me the job I had.

It gave me the man I love, and even if we don't have a future, I was married for a brief time to the one person on this planet who owns my heart.

CHAPTER FIFTY-FOUR

Graham

I STEP out of Lloyd's room even though all I want to do is shake him awake.

I know that Dr. Morgan will take the lead when it comes to convincing Lloyd that he needs the stent procedure, but I'm going to be chiming in.

I want Lloyd to live.

I want to know more about his son. I want to go to that scattering ground with him and just sit.

He needs to know that he's not alone. He's got me, and I hope to hell he has Trina.

I tug my phone out of my pocket.

I was warned not to use my phone on this ward. The nurse who wagged her finger at me told me to silence it. I did, but a glance through my missed calls and text messages tells me my wife hasn't tried to contact me.

"Dammit," I say, not giving a shit if the nurse overhears me. "Where are you, Trina?"

"I'm here."

I don't know if I'm fucking dreaming or not, but I turn at the sound of that soft voice.

"Graham," my wife says my name, and suddenly my world feels centered. "I'm so sorry."

I go to her. I don't care that she has two cups of coffee in her hands. I wrap my arms around her and hold her against me.

Then, I sob into her neck.

I cry for the pain I see on her face.

I cry for the tears streaming down her cheeks, and I cry for the man in bed who gave me my life.

He rescued me from the downward spiral I was in.

He sent me to a school where I met my best friends, and he gave me a job working alongside him.

The entire time he was helping me, he was burdened with a grief so profound it almost destroyed him. Then, another layer was added to that when he lost his wife.

"How…how is Mr. Abdon?" Trina stutters out.

I step back and grab both cups of coffee from her. "Come with me. He's asleep, but I know he'll want to see you when he wakes up."

Her hand on my forearm stalls me. "He won't. Something happened earlier. I don't know how much he told you."

"None of it," I say. "All I know is that he had your wedding rings. Please, Trina, come with me and tell me what's going on."

As another tear falls onto her cheek, she nods. "I'll tell you all of it."

———

TRINA STANDS next to Lloyd's hospital bed, staring down at him. "This is all my fault. He's going to die because of me."

I wrap my arms around her from behind to still her. She's shaking through a series of sobs.

"He's not going to die, Trina," I reassure her. "He needs a procedure. Once that's done, the doctor told me there's a strong chance that Lloyd will live for years."

She spins around to face me. "What?"

I skim a hand over her cheek to brush away her tears. "There's a partial blockage in one of the arteries that lead to his heart. He needs a cardiac stent to open it back up."

"Then he'll be okay?" her voice holds as much hope as her eyes.

I see what I feel when I look at her, relief and trust that what the doctor said is true. Lloyd isn't going anywhere. He's going to be a part of our lives for years to come.

I want Trina to be a part of my life forever, so I glance down at her hand. "Why did Lloyd have your wedding rings?"

She bites her bottom lip. "This isn't the time to talk about this, Graham. I don't think I should be here when he wakes up. I upset him."

She tugs free of my grasp and heads toward the door.

I'm on her heel before she makes it halfway there. I grab hold of her arm. "Stop, Trina. Please. I need to understand what the hell happened today."

Her head drops. "He went to the bakery to get a chocolate cake. He spoke to my mom about us. She told him he was wrong about us being married. She told him where I really live, Graham. He knew our marriage was fake."

I move around until I'm standing in front of her. "He confronted you about all of this?"

Her head shakes. "I went home...to the penthouse to see if I could explain things since you were in that meeting. It didn't go well."

"What happened?"

Her gaze meets mine, and I see defeat there. I see a broken spirit and endless sorrow swimming in her eyes. "He told me about your past. He told me about your mom."

I swallow back the pain that always hits me when I think of that day. It was the day I woke on the subway to find my mother gone. I never saw her again.

"Mr. Abdon was angry." She tugs on the sleeve of her blouse. "He assumed our fake marriage was your idea. I could see how much that pained him, so I told him I had come up with the plan. I explained that I suggested we get married and that I was the one who negotiated the payout."

"Trina."

She steps closer to me to cup her hands over my cheeks. "He loves you, Graham. I could see how much it hurt him that we had deceived him, so I wanted to spare you both that. It's better this way. I can walk away, and you can rebuild the bond you share with him."

It's so fucking admirable and selfless that I tear up for the goddamn umpteenth time today.

"Is that what you want?" I ask her bluntly. "Do you want a divorce, Trina? Do you want this to be over?"

She stands tall even though tears are streaming down her cheeks. "I want you to be happy. I want you to have Mr. Abdon in your life."

I stare into her stormy blue eyes. "What do you want? I want to know what you really want and don't make it about me, Trina. Be selfish. Tell me what would make you happy."

Her bottom lip quivers. "I can't say."

"Say it." I hear the plea in my tone. "I feel it. I just need you to say it. You were going to tell me tonight during our special dinner. I know you were."

"You were going to say it too," she says.

Her hands leap up to cup my wrists as I hold her face.

We stare at each other like that, each knowing what this moment means for us.

"I love you," I confess. "With everything I am, I fucking love you, Trina."

"I love you," she finally says the words to me. "I want to be your wife. I want that more than anything."

"We'll get married again." I kiss the corner of her mouth. "The right way this time with your family and Lloyd. He'll play the harmonica at the reception."

She nods. "I'll sign anything Morty No-Last-Name needs me to sign."

I laugh. "You don't need to sign a thing. You need to dance with me at our wedding and every anniversary party we're going to have."

She kisses my chin. "And we'll have a baby or two?"

"At least." I laugh. "We'll teach them how to love. We'll take them to the beach and cook hot dogs over an open fire…"

"And dip our toes in the water?"

"We'll help them grow into good people."

"Like us?" she asks.

"I haven't always been a good person," I confess. "I did things when I was young. I stole. I got into fights. I talked back."

"We all make mistakes, Graham." She looks me in the eye. "You've grown into an incredible, honorable man."

"I want to be a man that my wife can be proud of."

She presses her lips to mine for a soft kiss. "I am extremely proud of you, Graham Locke."

"I am too."

We both turn at the sound of Lloyd's voice.

"Lloyd?" I dart toward the bed. "You're awake."

Lloyd reaches up to trail a hand over the oxygen tube running into his nose. "I'm still here?"

"You're not going anywhere." I smile. "We need you too much."

"Trina," Mr. Abdon says my wife's name softly. "Come here. Come closer."

She does as he asks and takes a place standing next to me.

"I'm sorry." Lloyd looks at Trina. "I had no idea that you two had fallen in love."

"You heard us talking?" I ask. "You heard all of that?"

"Every word," he acknowledges with a curt nod before he looks at me. "Your wife took the blame to save our relationship, Bull. She did that for you."

I scoop my hand around Trina's waist. "I married the most incredible woman in the world, and as soon as you're back on your feet, we're having the wedding we never had."

"You don't have to hold off on my account."

I lean down to smooth a hand over Mr. Abdon's forehead. "We sure as hell do. You're my best man. I need you beside me when I marry my wife again."

CHAPTER FIFTY-FIVE

Trina

"I GREW UP IN FOSTER CARE." Graham glances at me as we wait in the corridor for Dr. Morgan to finish examining and speaking with Lloyd. "I aged out while in care. I was technically in the care of a couple at that time, but Lloyd and his wife paid for my tuition at The Buchanan School. I spent my summer and winter breaks working and splitting my time between my friends' homes. Sometimes, I'd stay with Lloyd and Sela for a few nights. Occasionally, I'd head back over to my foster parents' house to crash, but I lost touch with them over the years. I didn't have a real home or a family."

I step closer to him, so that I can wrap both my arms around him. "You do now. You have Lloyd and me. You're also an important part of the Shaw family even though most of them don't know it yet."

"You think your family is going to like me?"

I smile as I study his handsome face. "They will. I told my mom that I love you."

That earns me a deep kiss.

"Wow," I whisper when our lips part. "That was something else."

"You told your mom about me?" His face lights up. "Today?"

"Or yesterday?" I shrug. "I don't know what time it is, and I don't care."

"For once, I don't either." He laughs.

I trail a finger over his jaw. "You were afraid to tell me about your past. Why? Did you think I wouldn't understand?"

He scratches the side of his nose. "I was ashamed."

"You were put in a position no child should ever be in."

His lips brush against my forehead. "That's never an excuse for bad behavior. I met dozens of other kids who were in foster care too. I doubt like hell any of them did the shit I did. I broke into Abdons trying to find something to pawn for money to run away."

"To run away from your foster home?"

He glances toward the closed door of Lloyd's room. "My grandma lived in Philadelphia. I thought if I could get to her, she'd want to take me in."

My heart aches for the boy he used to be. I can't imagine feeling that alone. When I was growing up, I'd wish for moments alone, but I rarely got them. I'm grateful for that now. I didn't know how incredibly lucky I was to be surrounded by so much love.

"After I was arrested, Lloyd dropped the charges, but I had a sit-down with Peggy before I was released."

"Peggy? Judge Mycella? The judge who married us?"

"Yes." He smiles. "She worked in family court back then. She was the one who told me my grandmother wanted nothing to do with me."

"I'm sorry, Graham." I step closer to him. "I'm so sorry."

He drops his gaze. "Lloyd and Sela turned my life around. I was fifteen when we met. I don't know where I'd be today if it weren't for them."

"Lloyd is a good man," I reiterate.

Graham glances at me. "He's the best man I've ever known."

"You're like a son to him."

He shoves a hand through his hair. "I found out tonight that Lloyd had a son who died."

My gaze searches his face. "What?"

"The doctor let it slip." He locks eyes with me. "He said that Lloyd has been going to a memorial park in New Jersey to visit the spot where he scattered the ashes of his wife and his son."

"I didn't know," I whisper.

"Neither did I."

"He needs us, Graham." I take both his hands in mine. "He needs us to help him. We are his family."

"We are," he agrees. "Thank you for agreeing to marry me, Trina Shaw. You've brought so much to my life and Lloyd's life."

"Trina Locke," I correct him. "First thing tomorrow morning, I'm going to start the process to change my name to Trina Locke."

I GLANCE down when my phone vibrates in my hand. A nurse warned me to turn it off, but I wanted to keep it on in case Aurora or Eldon needed me.

Graham and I just watched Lloyd being taken to the operating room. He agreed to the procedure and to whatever else he needs to do to get better.

Now, it's a waiting game.

Dr. Morgan assured us the procedure wouldn't take long and that he'd have Lloyd back in his room once he spent some time in recovery.

"Is everything all right?" Graham asks from where he's standing next to me.

"I brought my friend to the emergency department earlier." I sigh. "She wasn't feeling well."

"You brought her into the ER here? Is she okay?"

"She found out tonight that she's pregnant," I tell him. "She's being discharged. Her boyfriend is texting me to ask if I want to see her before they leave the hospital."

Graham reaches for my hand. "Let's go."

"We should wait here for Lloyd." I don't move. "I think we need to be here in case Dr. Morgan has to talk to you."

He shakes his head. "I think Lloyd's procedure will go off without a hitch. Let's go see your friend."

I nod. "Can we do one thing first?"

"Anything." He perks a brow. "Do you want to find a supply closet for a not-so-quickie?"

Tapping my left hand on his chest, I laugh. "I want that, but the nurse will ban us from the hospital forever."

His gaze falls to my hand. "I think I know what you want."

Before I can say it, he's dropped to one knee in the middle of the corridor.

A collective gasp escapes the three nurses behind the desk.

"Trina, my beautiful wife. Please do me the honor of being my partner in life." His hand dives into his pocket to retrieve both rings. "Stay married to me forever. Have children with me. Let me do whatever I can to help you live the life you are meant to live. Let me love you every second of every hour of every day until we leave this earth."

Applause erupts before I can even say yes.

But I do.

I nod, yell out my answer, and cry as my husband slips my rings back on my finger before he dips me into a breathtaking kiss.

CHAPTER FIFTY-SIX

GRAHAM

MY WIFE HAS her rings back on her finger. My heart belongs to her. Lloyd is in surgery, and I'm on my way to meet Trina's friends.

I don't know how this night can get better, but it will.

Once Lloyd is back in his room and settled, I plan on taking Trina home.

I'll carry her over the threshold, drop her in bed and keep her there for hours.

I don't know how it's possible that I've become this fortunate.

I'm a lucky bastard, and I'll never forget it.

As we wait for the elevator to take us down to the emergency department, Trina glances at me. "You got that tattoo on your arm to cover your bull tattoo, didn't you?"

Lloyd must have spilled those beans earlier, but I'm not mad.

My life is an open book now. I want Trina to know everything there is to know about me.

"I got the bull tattoo when I was thirteen."

"Is that legal?"

"Not even a little bit." I laugh. "I was placed in a home with another kid who was seventeen. He knew a guy who did tattoos in the back of a pancake restaurant."

She holds in a laugh. "That should have been your first clue that it was a bad idea."

"You think?" I quip. "Anyways, I gave him twenty bucks, and he gave me a tattoo that I thought was cool at the time."

She purses her lips. "I'd give almost anything to see that bull tattoo."

The elevator dings signaling its arrival on our floor, so I lean close and press my lips to her ear. "Blow me, and I'll show you a picture."

She turns to lock her eyes on mine. "Deal."

I trail her as she boards the elevator and presses the button for the main floor. "Being married to you is the best adventure I've ever had, Graham. I can't wait for the future."

I reach for her hand, draw it up to my lips and kiss it. "Being married to you is the greatest gift I've ever been given."

"I'M ELDON BRECKTON." A brown-haired guy in a police officer's uniform shakes my hand. "It's good to meet you, sir."

I may have a few years on him, but I don't fall into that category. "It's Graham. Call me Graham."

He gives me a curt nod before he shifts his attention back to Trina. "Thanks again for bringing her in."

Trina smiles. "I'm glad I was there. How is she?"

"She's great." He beams with a broad smile. "She's getting dressed. I told her I'd order an Uber to get us home. We're both tired as hell, but happy. She told me you know, Trina. You know about the baby."

Trina nods her head. "I know."

Eldon huffs out a laugh. "A baby, Trina. How fucking awesome is that?"

She wraps her arms around him for a hug. "I'm so happy for you both."

He pats the center of Trina's back. "I asked her to marry me tonight. I never expected to do it in a hospital, but life is full of surprises, right?"

"Graham asked me to marry him tonight too." Trina waves her left hand in the air. "We're actually already married."

"You got married tonight?" He huffs out a laugh. "When? Where?"

"No." Trina chuckles. "We've been married for a while. It's a long story, but it's time everyone I care about knows that I married the most amazing man in the world."

Eldon's gaze wanders past my shoulder. "There she is. Look how beautiful she is."

I turn to glance at his fiancée.

The sight of her smiling face floods me with memories.

For the first time in my life, I don't run when I see someone I used to know from foster care.

I've crossed streets to avoid people I recognize from when I was a kid. I once handed off a meeting to someone else because the person I was supposed to sit down with was a woman I'd spent two months in a foster home with when she was ten and I was twelve.

I've avoided my past, but that's done.

That stops now.

The woman approaching us slows. "Oh my god. Graham? Is that you?"

"Ro Sherman," I whisper her name before I take off in a sprint toward her.

She leaps into my arms the same way she did when she was a seven-year-old kid. "I can't believe you're here."

I set her down on her feet and look her over.

The shy girl I used to make ham and cheese sandwiches for is now a young woman. The gap between her two front teeth is gone, but the mole just below the corner of her right eye is still there. "I'm here. I'm here with Trina."

She glances behind me to where I know her fiancé and my wife are standing. "You know Trina?"

"I'm her husband."

"What?" Her hands reach for mine. "I'm so lost right now."

Those words resonate because the last time I saw her, she was standing on the stoop of a house in Queens with a doll in her hand and a pink ribbon in her hair. She was crying as we waved goodbye to each other.

We'd known each other for almost a year, but we were being split apart that day. She was heading to a new foster home. I was being taken to another.

Trina moves to stand next to me. "This is my boss, Aurora. He's my husband now too."

"You're Trina's boss?" Her gaze searches my face. "She told me his name was Mr. Locke. I never asked his first name. I never knew your surname. You were always just Graham to me."

"You were Ro to me."

"I can't believe it's you." She takes a deep breath. "After all this time. I can't believe you remember me."

I huff out a laugh. "You can't believe I remember you? I was a teenager the last time I saw you. You were seven. It's unreal that you remember me."

"How could I forget you?" She pats the center of my chest. "You made my school lunches. You always gave me both pieces of ham and cheese on my sandwich. You'd take mustard sandwiches to school so that I would have more to eat."

I'd do it again in a heartbeat.

"Are you happy?" I question her. "I always wondered what happened to you."

She smiles. "I was adopted when I was nine. I have two older brothers and the most incredible parents. They've all been so good to me."

"Good." I press a kiss to the center of her forehead.

"I finally felt as though I belonged somewhere when the Saliks adopted me." Her voice is quiet. "I hope you found that too."

"I did," I say as my gaze drifts to Trina's face. "It took a long time, but I found the place I belong, and I've never been happier."

CHAPTER FIFTY-SEVEN

Graham

"THE PROCEDURE WENT OFF WITHOUT A HITCH," Dr. Morgan tells me. "I want to keep Lloyd here for the day for observation."

"Can we see him?" I glance to where Trina is standing in the doorway of Lloyd's room.

She's been quiet since we said goodbye to Aurora and Eldon. We agreed to meet up with them in a few days for dinner.

The plan is to celebrate – everything.

That includes their engagement, our marriage, and their baby.

It's hard to wrap my mind around the fact that the last time I saw Ro, she was a seven-year-old kid, and soon, she'll be a mom.

"Why don't you go in and say hello, then give him a few hours to rest?" Dr. Morgan suggests. "By then, he'll be feeling a lot better. We'll have him up and on his feet before the end of the day."

"That fast?" Trina turns back to ask.

"Movement is essential." He nods. "He's got some work to do in terms of managing stress and his diet. We'll need to get him on an exercise regime, but that can be worked out over the coming weeks. I'm going to set you up with some information regarding all of that."

"Thank you." I extend a hand to him. "You saved his life."

"I did my job." He smiles as he shakes my hand. "Lloyd is a good man. I'm glad I could help."

"I'M GOING to give you two some time alone." Trina takes a step back from where she's been standing next to Lloyd's bed. "Graham and I will be back in a few hours, Mr. Abdon."

"Lloyd," he stresses. "I'm Lloyd, and you're Mrs. Locke."

"I am." She smiles. "I'm putting the wheels in motion to become Mrs. Locke legally."

That brings a grin to Lloyd's face. "Will you bring me back something from our library to read?"

"How about A Fool's Grace?" Trina wiggles her brows. "It's our favorite."

"It is." He reaches for her hand.

She takes it in hers. "I'm sorry again for everything."

"That brought us here, and this is a good place." His gaze drifts to my face. "Isn't that right, Graham?"

"That's right."

"I'll be in the corridor." Trina kisses my cheek. "Take as

much time as you need but remember the doctor wants Lloyd to rest so…"

"So make it quick?" I chuckle.

"We have years to talk." Trina's gaze volleys from my face to Lloyd's. "Years to make memories together."

I nod as I watch her leave the room, clicking the door shut behind her.

"Sit, Graham." Lloyd points at a chair next to the bed. "I need to say something."

"It can wait," I insist. "I'll be back in a few hours after you've had time to rest."

"Sit." His voice is more determined. "I need to say this now. It's long overdue."

I tug the chair forward until it's directly in Lloyd's line of sight. Then, I unbutton my suit jacket and lower myself down.

He takes a heavy breath. "I haven't been honest with you, Graham."

Crossing my arms over my chest, I shake my head. "You're the most honest man I've ever met, Lloyd."

"I didn't just come to New York to wrap up my business," he admits. "I came to see my family."

I nod. "I understand."

"Do you?" he questions in a soft tone. "Because I don't."

I lean forward. "What do you mean?"

He swallows hard. "I promised Sela that I'd live in Paris after she died. I told her I didn't belong there without her, but she insisted that I live in the flat we had bought five years ago. She wanted me to explore all the places she longed to see. She felt my being there would help me feel closer to her, but I felt so damn empty. I felt so alone."

I don't respond. He doesn't need that from me. I know

him well enough to know when there are things he has to get off his chest.

"We had a boy, Graham." His voice breaks. "Lloyd Junior."

LJ.

"He passed when he was fourteen." He rubs his eyes. "It was cancer. It was aggressive, and there was nothing anyone could do for him."

"I'm sorry," I say sincerely. "I'm so fucking sorry, Lloyd."

"It happened years before we met you." He glances down at his hands. "It shattered Sela. I felt as though a part of me died with him and we just existed. It was day by day, hour by hour for a long time, and then you were there."

I nod. "I broke into the store."

"You broke through our fog." He chuckles. "You were a little older than LJ was when he died but so different than him. Sela and I were lost. You were lost, so we decided to help you."

"I'm forever grateful to you both."

"I knew when I found you in the store that I had to do something for you," he says. "At first, I think it was just about that. We saw a troubled boy in need, and we wanted to lend a hand."

I don't have words, so I stay silent and let him continue.

He glances toward the window. "It became more to me when you were just shy of your seventeenth birthday."

"What do you mean, Lloyd?"

He pats the bed. "Give me your hand, Bull."

I take his shaking hand in mine.

"I wanted you to be my son." His eyes well with unshed tears. "I wanted you to be Graham Abdon. I felt that in my heart. It wasn't about LJ anymore at that point. It was about you. You cleaned up your act. You were making your grades. You were someone I was proud of."

I tear up too. "That was all because of you."

"Sela couldn't do it," he whispers. "She felt it might be a betrayal to LJ if we adopted you. She loved you, Bull, but in her heart, there was just enough room for him."

I squeeze his hand, touched that he shared something so incredibly personal with me. "I'm honored that you even considered the idea, Lloyd."

"You may not be my son on paper, but you are my boy." His tears fall. "I want to be there for you and your wife. I want to meet your children one day, and I want to sign the company over to you."

"You're going to be around for years to tell me how to run it." I laugh through my tears. "The first step is getting you rested so we can get you out of here. Then, I'd like to go to New Jersey with you. I want to sit with you in the place where Sela and LJ are resting."

"I'd like that," he says through a sob. "I'd like that a lot."

CHAPTER FIFTY-EIGHT

TRINA

"I CAN MAKE something for us to eat," I say as we step off the elevator and into our penthouse. We left the hospital and headed straight home to rest and recharge.

We'll go back in a few hours after Lloyd has had a chance to rest.

Graham shakes his head. "I'm craving my wife."

I laugh. "You want to have sex? You have energy for that after the night we just had?"

"We are alone in this big penthouse." He slowly unknots his tie and slips it off. "I can fuck my wife anywhere I choose."

I kick off one shoe sending it flying to the left before the other one follows it. "Where will we start?"

"I'll fuck you here on the floor." He perks a brow as he drops his suit jacket.

"You're that desperate for me?" My fingers grip the zipper on my skirt, sending it down.

"I'm always desperate for you." He smirks as he makes quick work of the buttons on his shirt.

It slides from his shoulders.

I step closer to look at the tattoo on his arm. "I can't believe that beneath all those lines and bands of ink there's a bull."

"That's right." He drops his hands to his belt. "I believe we had an agreement. I'd show you a picture of my old tattoo, and you'd wrap those gorgeous lips of yours around my dick."

I slide a fingertip over my bottom lip. "I'm ready if you are."

He looks me over. "You're not ready. Strip, Trina."

I quickly lose my skirt and blouse until I'm standing barefoot wearing nothing but a white bra and a pair of pink lace panties.

"Let's renegotiate," Graham says as he yanks his belt free.

"I liked the deal we struck earlier." My hands dart to my hips. "One blow job for a picture of your tattoo."

"One long and slow pussy eating session for a peek at that picture."

The corners of my lips lift into a smile. "I get to see your tattoo, and you'll eat me out?"

"I love eating you out, dear."

I step closer to him. "Let's compromise."

He drops his pants. His boxer briefs follow, leaving him naked and very aroused.

I glance down. "Please, darling. Compromise for me."

His fist circles his cock, giving it a long stroke. "Name it, Trina. I would do anything for you."

I stare into his eyes. "You mean that, don't you?"

His hand darts to my face. He cups my cheek. "I mean it

with everything that I am. I would do anything for you. Anything."

I reach back to unclasp my bra. "Will you love, honor and cherish me all the days of your life?"

"I do." He skims a finger over the waistband of my panties. "Will you love me in sickness and in health? For richer or poorer?"

"I do." I tilt my chin. "You're not going to ruin my panties again, are you?"

He lets out a low chuckle. "We're in the middle of negotiating. I can't promise that."

I reach down to take his cock in my palm. "If you show me the picture of your bull tattoo, I'll sit on your face while I suck this."

"Good god, woman."

I laugh. "Is that a yes? Do you agree to those terms?"

"I agree." He moves in to kiss me. "I'll get the picture. You get rid of the panties before I rip them to shreds."

I move quickly to slide them from my body.

He rakes me from head to toe. "Jesus. I'll meet you in our bedroom in one minute."

"One minute?" I look at my watch. "Your time starts now, Mr. Locke."

He sets off in a sprint down the corridor to the east wing.

I can't keep my eyes off of his spectacular naked ass. "I love you!"

Glancing back over his shoulder, he calls out to me, "I love you. I fucking love you, and I always will!"

EPILOGUE

THREE MONTHS LATER

Graham

"THANK fuck Lloyd didn't get Bette to cater this." Graham laughs. "Look at this, Trina. Look at all these people we love."

She reaches for my hand. "It's incredible, isn't it?"

We're at Howerton House. It's one of the premier event venues in Manhattan.

Trina and I wanted a ceremony in the penthouse with a catered dinner for our friends and family, but Lloyd wanted more.

It was his idea to rent out the garden terrace for the day.

Peggy was on hand to marry us again.

Lloyd stood up next to me. Trina chose her sister Falon to be her matron-of-honor.

I'd met her and her husband Asher at a small gathering for Ro's birthday.

Asher sang two songs.

Ro was in heaven as she danced with her fiancé.

It was a good night and the start of our journey to telling everyone in Trina's life that she's a married woman.

Her dad was ecstatic. Her siblings were excited for her. Her brother, George, had a few questions for me, but he's come around.

I glance over to see him sitting at a table with his wife, alongside Sean and Harrison, who both came without plus ones. George lifts a beer bottle in greeting in the air. I toss him a wave.

"It's too bad that Kavan couldn't make it," Trina says quietly.

We spent time with Kavan last night in the private dining room at Sérénité. He toasted to our future and never once mentioned the past.

His story belongs to him, so I haven't shared that with my wife.

On the way home, I explained that he'd been through hell and fought his way back. She assured me that his secrets are his to tell and if he ever wants to, she'll be there to listen.

"Aurora looks beautiful tonight." Trina points to where Ro and Eldon are sitting. "She's got that pregnancy glow."

I drop my gaze to the lace gown Trina is wearing. "She's no match for you. You took my breath away when you came down the aisle with your parents."

"You stole mine the first time you ordered me to marry you."

I laugh. "I persuaded you, Trina."

That day feels like a lifetime ago. So much has changed.

We've fallen in love and married for a second time now.

Lloyd has been talking about transferring ownership of Abdons to me, but I'm in no rush. I work the job he hired me to work, and he comes into the office a few times a month to weigh in.

He's been spending much of his time moving into an apartment in Brooklyn. It's a fresh start for him in the neighborhood he grew up in.

"It's almost time for dinner." Trina kisses my jaw. "Then speeches, dancing, and we get to cut our wedding cake."

"Then I can take my wife home and carry her over the threshold?"

She glides her lips to my neck to pepper a line of soft kisses there. "I can't wait for that."

"I'M GOING to accept the position in marketing that Hank offered me," Trina says as she walks back into our bedroom carrying a small plate and a fork. "You'll need to start looking for a new assistant."

I take in how utterly beautiful she is. She looks satisfied because she is.

As soon as we exited the elevator in our penthouse, our clothes were off. Her wedding dress is on the floor in the foyer next to my tuxedo. I lost my boxer briefs outside the door of our bedroom. Her lingerie is at the foot of our bed.

We spent more than two hours making love. It was two of the best hours of my life, and I can't wait to take her again.

I don't hold back my smile even though I'm going to miss having her within my view all day at the office. "I'm proud of you."

She takes a small bite of the chocolate cake that's on the

plate. It's a piece of our wedding cake. Her mom packed it up for us at the reception before she sent us home.

"Whoever your new assistant is, be kind to them, Graham." She carefully crawls onto the bed to straddle me while balancing the cake in her hand.

"I'm kind."

Shaking her head, she smiles. "Promise me you'll never have another angry a.m. or pissy p.m. again."

"What the fuck is that?" I bark out a laugh. "Are those real things?"

"In your world they are," she says as she feeds me a bite of the cake. "I have to admit you haven't had either one in a long time."

"That's because my wife keeps me well-fucked and happy."

"Speaking of well-fucked." She glances down at her nude body. "This was a much better wedding night than our first one."

"The night is not over yet, Mrs. Locke." I take another offered bite of cake from her.

Joy swims in her expression. "Have I told you how much I love being Trina Locke?"

She's told me countless times, but I'll never tire of it. "Have I told you how much I love being married to you?"

She scoops up another small piece of the cake to slide it between her lips. "Tell me again."

I skim my hands over her bare thighs. My cock is hard again, so I push her back slightly so she can feel what she's doing to me.

Her eyes widen. "Your cock likes being married to me."

I huff out a laugh. "My heart loves it even more. I can't wait for tomorrow, Trina, and the day after that."

"All the days to come," she adds. "All the adventures we'll have."

I take a leap of faith because although I can't read my wife's mind, I know her. I know what she's been dreaming about recently. I know what she wants.

"In the brownstone in Brooklyn," I whisper.

The plate in her hand shakes. "Graham?"

"I saw the listing for it on the laptop in the study," I confess.

"I thought I cleared the history." She laughs. "I was just browsing."

I motion for her to feed me another bite of cake. "You were thinking about our future."

She carefully slides the fork between my lips. "It's all I think about."

"Our children," I say with a tremor in my voice.

"All of our children." She leans forward to press a kiss on my cheek. "I know we've talked about kids, and we agreed to wait for a year or two to have a baby, but there's something else, Graham. I think we should consider…"

"Adoption," I finish her sentence. "We'll have a baby when we're ready, and we'll adopt too."

Tears fill her eyes almost instantly. "Yes. I want that so much."

It's what I want too.

"There are so many older children," she says on a stuttered breath. "We have a lot of love to give."

I reach up to cup her face in my hands. "That brownstone in Brooklyn is made for our future family, Trina. It's two blocks from Dobb's. Lloyd lives within walking distance of it. There's a library there so we can move all the books from here to there. Your mom and Lloyd will love that."

I gave her mom a keycard to our penthouse two months

ago. She calls it her *private library card*. She stops by whenever she's in need of a new read and some time with her daughter.

"They would love that so much," she agrees softly.

"I called the listing agent for the brownstone." I run my hands up to her waist. "We have an appointment to see it tomorrow morning before we head out to Westhampton Beach for our honeymoon."

"You're way ahead of me on this." She lets out a soft laugh.

I've been planning the future since the first time she said *I do*.

She moves to place the empty plate on the nightstand.

I can't help but lick a path over her left nipple as she reaches past me.

That lures a soft moan from her. "I love you, Graham."

"I love you, Trina." I tug her closer to me, wrapping my arms around her. "I can't wait for every single one of our tomorrows."

ALSO BY DEBORAH BLADON
& SUGGESTED READING ORDER

The Obsessed Series

The Exposed Series

The Pulse Series

Impulse

The Vain Series

Solo

The Ruin Series

The Gone Series

Fuse

The Trace Series

Chance

The Ember Series

The Rise Series

Haze

Shiver

Torn

The Heat Series

Risk

melt

The Tense Duet

Sweat

Troublemaker

Worth

Hush

Bare

Wish

Sin

Lace

Thirst

Compass

Versus

Ruthless

Bloom

Rush

Catch

Frostbite

Xoxo

He Loves Me Not

Bittersweet

The Blush Factor

BULL

THANK YOU

Thank you for purchasing and downloading my book. I can't even begin to put to words what it means to me. If you enjoyed it, please remember to write a review for it. Let me know your thoughts! I want to keep my readers happy.

For more information on new series and standalones, please visit my website, deborahbladon.com. There are book trailers and other goodies to check out.

Feel free to reach out to me! I love connecting with all of my readers because without you, none of this would be possible.

Thank you, for everything.

ABOUT THE AUTHOR

Deborah Bladon has never read a romance hero she didn't like. Her love for romance novels began when she was old enough to board the bus, library card in hand to check out the newest Harlequin paperbacks. She's a Canadian by heart, and by passport, but you can often spot her in New York City sipping a latte and looking for inspiration for her next story. Manhattan is definitely her second home.

She cherishes her family and believes that each day is a gift for writing, for reading, and for loving.

Printed in Great Britain
by Amazon

87367024R00173